SAVING
COOPER

MAGGIE LOCKE

authorHOUSE®

AuthorHouse™
1663 Liberty Drive
Bloomington, IN 47403
www.authorhouse.com
Phone: 1 (800) 839-8640

This is a work of fiction. All of the characters, names, incidents, organizations, and dialogue in this novel are either the products of the author's imagination or are used fictitiously.

Published by AuthorHouse 09/07/2017

ISBN: 978-1-5246-7472-4 (sc)
ISBN: 978-1-5246-7474-8 (hc)
ISBN: 978-1-5246-7473-1 (e)

Library of Congress Control Number: 2017903426

Print information available on the last page.

This book is printed on acid-free paper.

This is dedicated to my Dad, Ed Noyer,
you are loved and missed.

CONTENTS

CHAPTER ONE

1850 PITTSBURGH, PENNSYLVANIA

Amanda Green sat on the window seat of her pink and white striped bedroom reading the letter her maid May had brought to her, she read it again surprised by the words, her Cousin Jonathan McClure, wanted her to visit and possibly marry his son Mervin, her memories of Mervin were of him tying cans to her dogs' tail and chasing him with a torch while she cried and screamed for him to stop.

He shook her blond head to clear it of the disturbing memory.

She stood tapping the letter against the palm of her hand, she looked out the window, the pink and white striped curtains blowing in the slight summer breeze, her green eyes searched the green hillside for the lone grave, seeing it her breath caught in her throat DA she thought her brave Irish father, she remembered him telling her how he came to America almost penniless, how he worked as a shoe shine boy and then a factory worker and then how he met Malcolm Sinclair in the pub and found out that he was in the indigo business and looking for a partner, now Mr. Sinclair was dead and so was her beloved father, now she Amanda Green was the sole heir to the indigo fortune.

A tear slid out of her emerald green eye moving wetly down her cheek, she brushed it away, breathing hard.

Amanda composed herself fixing her hair, she placed her hands on either side of her cheeks as she stared at her reflection in the mirror on her nightstand, she looked terrible and her mother would know she'd been crying, she poured out water from the pitcher soaking the washcloth in the cool water, she sighed feeling better.

She looked at herself in the mirror again satisfied and went to see her mother.

Honey Beatrice McClure Green sat in the red and gold wingback chair looking over the dinner menu, she set the pen down thinking dreamily about Hillcrest her cousin's home in Virginia, how exciting Amanda her Amanda was going to be mistress of Hillcrest one of the largest and finest plantations around, well she'd make sure that Amanda didn't mess up such an opportunity.

Amanda entered the library, her mother looked at her smiling, Amanda handed her mother the letter which she read, and Honey looked up with that same cat that swallowed the canary look as she said "What an opportunity isn't it wonderful to be mistress of Hillcrest as you know it's one of the finest plantations around, Jonathan wrote to me and asked about you, you being of marriageable age and I thought it was a good match" Honey said enthusiastically "This might be the best thing for you my dear, you've been so sad, you need to go to parties and dance and meet interesting people" Honey said dreamily, "I can't go to parties we're in mourning and I certainly can't marry, Da died three months ago, really Mother" Amanda said shocked and exasperated "Well I thought of that too my dear we can tell our neighbors that you've been betrothed from birth and they will and they know that Mervin is your cousin and that he's family and I'm sure that they've been mourning too, so it will be a happy occasion in the midst of all the sadness" Honey said cheerily, "Oh mother I don't believe you, Da would never agree to this …..this scheme if he were alive and you know it" Amanda said appalled, "But he's not here is he, we have to do what we have to do don't we" Honey said frivolously, "Well I don't have to marry Mervin, Da gave me enough money that I don't have to marry at all if I don't want to, I'm his heir "Amanda said angrily, "Oh but Mervin was such a lovely boy, such a gentleman" Honey said sweetly hoping to change to a more pleasant topic, "He was not Mother, not to me anyway, he use to torture my dog, poor Buford" she said through clenched teeth, "Oh that smelly dog, I'm so glad he's gone always tracking mud onto my nice clean floors, and anyway Amanda you want to marry I know you do" Honey said lightly and Amanda frowned "Yes, I want to marry, but I don't and I won't marry Mervin McClure mother" Amanda said bluntly with that she left the table grabbing her shawl she headed out the door, as she stood on the stone steps she choked back a sob her Da wouldn't do this to her, he really loved her.

She turned walking pass the manicured flower garden and up the hill towards the shady willow tree, she stood in front of the gray slate stone that bore the name in bold black letters SHAMUS ANTHONY GREEN.

From behind her she heard the swishing of skirts, she turned to see her maid May, May fidgeted nervously hopping from foot to foot, her freckled face flushed with excursion

"Miss, Miss your mother asked me to come find you, she wants to see you, how exciting Miss Amanda, you're getting married your father would be pleased I imagine you really miss him and would've wanted him to walk you down the aisle" May said cheerily, "Thank you May, so when are you going to visit your sister" Amanda said conversationally and also to try to change the subject, "Next week Miss and you'll be gone too whatever will your mother do" May said with a smile, "All the parties and such what is it that they call them in the south?" May asked excitedly Amanda smiled at her enthusiasm "Cotillions, but Mother and I are in mourning I can't go to parties and such even if I wanted to mourning lasts a year" Amanda said "But Mrs. Green said you were going to Virginia?" May questioned "I know "Amanda said quietly "But I really don't want to marry Mervin and I'm trying to get out of it so I'm hoping Mother will come to her senses" Mays' doe brown eyes widened and her small cherry mouth dropped into an O, she blinked saying quietly "So what are you going to do Miss Amanda?" Amanda's brow furrowed "Well if she makes me go than I will have to make myself so insufferable that Mervin will have no choice, but to send me home" "Do you think that will work Miss, your mother said he was such a nice man with good manners" May said confused Amanda laughed "No he's not or at least he wasn't when I knew him, he used to torture my dog and dip my hair in the ink well and eat all the cookies and blame it on me, I don't want to marry him, but I don't seem to have a choice Mother has fixed it all up in a bow" Amanda said dejected.

The two women reached the house walking in the door, Honey paced in the parlor, her heels clicking against the mahogany floor as she stepped off the Chinese styled flowered rug, Amanda paused in the doorway she took a deep breath as she entered the parlor, "You were at his grave again, I don't know why you insist on going up there really I don't" Honey said curtly "Did you love Da Mother?" asked quietly Honey turned away frowning "I thought I did, your father and I were just too different and I thought by marrying an Irishman that I was wild and scandalous, but it died, but I have you my dear and I promised myself that you would marry a man worthy of you and I 've deemed that man to be Mervin, Mervin is a southern gentleman born and raised with good southern values, I should have married a southerner" Honey stated flatly "MOTHER" Amanda shouted she shook with rage "I don't believe you, did Da have any idea how you really felt" Amanda said through her tears "Yes, he knew, but he was a Catholic so divorce was out of the question, but then you came a long and you were our world so all the love we once felt for each other went to you" Amanda shook her head saying "I can't ……..I can't ………I can't deal with this it's too big why are you dumping this on my shoulders now, what if the same thing happens I won't stay I'll leave" Honey kissed her wet cheek saying quietly "You'll do your duty" Amanda pulled away from her running for the stairs blinded by her tears, once she reached the safety of her room she felt that she could breathe again, she looked around her room at all the things she ever loved, the canapé always made her feel so elegant, now as she flopped onto that very canapé bed hugging the pillow she began to cry again in earnest.

The next few weeks went by swiftly as everything was arranged for Amanda's own trip. Rufus the coach driver pulled the carriage up in front of the red brick mansion, Wilson the aging Butler carried the trunks securing them to the top of the carriage, Amanda walked out the door her back ramrod straight, she was dressed in her emerald green riding habit in her hand was the carpet bag her father had given her for her twelfth birthday clutched tightly in her gloved hand.

"Amanda" her mother said as she came out to stand on the stone steps, she turned at her mother's voice, "What Mother" Amanda said irritably, her mother patted the at the mass of graying honey gold hair as she said "Amanda I just want what's best for you, I want you to marry well" "I know you do Mother, but I should have a say in my own future, it's not fair for you to run my life, I want a say" Amanda said frowning, "Well have a good trip dear" Honey sweetly "Thank you Mother" Amanda said flatly as she stepped into the carriage, she adjusted her skirts as the carriage pulled out of the circular drive and onto the busy cobblestoned streets of Pittsburgh.

After many days of travel the carriage swerved around a twisty dirt road towards the white washed pillared mansion as the carriage stopped in front she noticed the sweet smell of roses as they climbed up one side of the mansion.

She noticed the sprawling cotton fields with people hard at work in them, she turned her attention back to the house, it was then that she noticed the tall man with the graying brown hair standing on the steps, his beard neatly trimmed, he leaned heavily on the oak cane as he reached the door of the carriage she noticed that his eyes were a marry blue, "Amanda my dear how good it is to see you and how kind it is of you to accept our invitation, Mervin come say hello to your cousin," Mervin stood his doughy physique was accented by the ill- fitting blue coat he was wearing, he stared at the pretty petite blond and instantly felt a jolt of lust, he grinned wolfishly at the thought of having this delectable creature in his bed, he wondered if he could get her in bed before the wedding, he'd certainly try, she had to be better than the whores he was bedding.

Mervin walked down the steps, he was heavy jowled, his piggy nose sniffed anxiously as he drew near, she smelled of sunshine and wildflowers, he bent kissing her hand "So nice to see you again Amanda" as he tried to hide his lustful thoughts, "Won't you have some lemonade" he said flirtatiously "Thank you Mervin, I'd love some lemonade after such a long trip" they walked up the steps to the oaken table, they sat on the wide porch sipping the sweet and tart liquid, Amanda looked over at the carriage as a tall dark haired man carried one of the trunks as he passed the porch she looked into the bluest eyes she'd ever seen, he flushed as he stared at her, his skin the color coffee and cream, his full wide mouth quirked up in a half smile, she smiled back as she started to stand up, Mervin pushed the chair back, the chair grating across the white marble floor "COOPER" he shouted angrily, Cooper jerked in surprise turning as he said "Yes Sir Massa" "Take the ladies trunks and put them in her rooms" Mervin said seething, Cooper walked passed taking the trunks up the servants entrance, he thought about the blond haired woman and how she lowered her eyes when Massa Mervin yelled at him, he smiled thinking she was obviously interested in him as he with her, he carried the trunk with the carpet bag hanging off two long fingers.

They chatted presently through the afternoon, Amanda stood straightening her lilac colored gown "Well him sure you'd like to freshen up before dinner, so I'll show you to your rooms, I've assigned a girl to be your maid her name his Lilly" McClure said gently Amanda smiled "Thank you so much cousin Jonathan, I'm sure Lilly and I will get on marvelously," Amanda said anxious to get away from Mervin and his lustfulness.

McClure showed her to her rooms as she entered she saw her trunks and they were open as she walked closer she noticed some of her clothing and shoes were missing, she straightened up as the door opened that led to the adjoining room opened and a small fragile looking girl appeared her hair caught up in a red bandana, wisps of dark curly hair escaped, her eyes a sapphire blue, she curtsied saying quietly "Morning miss, sho are glad to have you here the Massas' have been in a frenzy to make everything all pretty for you, by the way my name is Lilly"" I'm Amanda Green, it's so nice to meet you Lilly, I hope we can be friends" Amanda said smiling, Lilly frowned thoughtfully as she said "I'm a slave Miss Amanda all I'll ever be is a slave so I don't see how we can be friends", Lilly turned away finishing the unpacking, Amanda's mouth dropped open, she snapped it shut with a snap as she said shocked "Slave, but oh no my cousin is a slave owner, I can't believe it", Lilly reached into the pocket of her apron pulling out the smelling salts, "You relax Miss Amanda I've the salts should you need them" Lilly said as she moved about the room, "Would like a soothing cup of Chamomile tea?" Lilly said trying to distract her from the news she'd received "No, no thank you Lilly" Amanda said distracted.

Cooper took the tray of lemonade off the porch taking it into the kitchen where he placed the tray on the cupboard, he turned grabbing a cookie from the tray on the table, he munched on the sweet oatmeal raisin cookie as he walked around Della's kitchen, he remembered sitting in the kitchen as a child when his mother was alive, she worked as a kitchen slave as well the Massas' favorite, then he thought about Amanda Green and the cookie suddenly tasted like sawdust in his mouth, he closed his eyes against the memory and the attraction, she was beautiful with her long blond hair and big green eyes and her creamy white skin, but she was off limits she was going to be the Big missy here so he better get his mind straight.

The bell rang and Cooper left the kitchen as he got close to the Library he heard the Massas' talking "When we have her money all our problems will be over, is Honey clear about that do you think?" McClure said as he puffed on a cigar then he leaned back in the chair "But I still get to bed her right?" Mervin asked concerned his Father laughed "Of course my boy of course" Mervin grinned greedily as he said "Good", Cooper brought in the decanter of whisky "Put it on the table" Mervin said Cooper bent placing the tray on the table, Mervin moved like a striking snake catching Cooper across the mouth his eyes watered and his nose stung, Mervin stood suddenly shouting" You looked at her, don't you ever look at her like that again or I'll kill you dead I swear it" Cooper backed up during the tirade the heel of his shoe caught the corner of a chair sending him to the floor, Cooper sat down hard his teeth clicking together audibly, he looked up at Massa Mervin with a look of scared surprise, he blinked then wiping a hand under his nose seeing blood, he stood with his head lowered saying quietly "Yes Massa, I won't trouble your Big Missy none" "Well wonders never cease I guess you were right Daddy, Cooper can be cooperative I didn't think so, go on boy git", Cooper bowed slightly saying" Yes Massa" he turned walking back to the kitchen, as he walked in Della turned "What happened Cooper" Della exclaimed she grabbed a rag and waddled over to where Cooper stood "Sit yourself down like a good lad" Della said good naturedly, Cooper pulled out two chairs sitting in one while Della shifted her massive frame to fit in the other, she dabbed lightly as his split lip, blood dripped slowly from his nose onto the rag, she dabbed at his bloody nose as Rhea the kitchen girl came in, she looked shyly at Cooper, she'd always had a crush on Cooper, but he'd never seemed interested in her, the shy girl emptied the contents of her apron onto the counter, she picked up the knife and began to peel potatoes.

Amanda came down the curved staircase with Lilly in her wake, Lilly held the white lace parasol while Amanda adjusted the straw bonnet with the green and white flowered dress swirled around her slim ankles, the McClure men saw her and came out of the Library "Where are you off to my dear" McClure drawled "Lilly told me that there are a number of gardens so I thought I'd walk in the gardens, oh by the way I hope you don't mind, but I've decided to make Lilly my companion" Amanda said brightly "She's not trained for that, she's a kitchen girl" Mervin said tartly "Well I can train her, she'll do fine won't you Lilly" Amanda said smartly, Amanda turned away in a swirl of skirts and blond hair as she flounced off in the direction of the gardens, Lilly looked frightened as she looked at both the Massas', she swallowed then ran after Amanda.

"Do you think you can tame her son, she's a feisty one" McClure said with raised eyebrows, Mervin smiled greedily then he licked his flabby lips" I believe I can tame the little filly and I know just the tool to use" both men laughed, Cooper peered around the corner standing stalk still knowing full well that the Massa's could be cruel, but he remembered the warmth of her smile and the powerful attraction he felt he couldn't let them hurt her so he listened to their plans, "When I have her money I can pay off the debt and we can stop selling slaves" McClure said with conspiratorial smile "And I can have her in my bed" Mervin said lustfully the two men walked back into the Library sitting down "Honey told me that her father spoiled and indulged her since birth and she's been trying unsuccessfully to marry her off, don't mess this up this will work if you don't mess it up" McClure said sternly, Mervin's eyes widened he knew his father's' temper he could be lethal when he wanted to be, "I won't mess it up Daddy I promise" Mervin said frightened "Good, see that you don't" McClure said as he squeezed Mervin's' flabby chin.

Amanda grumbled as she walked out the door, Lilly scurried out the door behind her breathing hard "Wait Miss Amanda wait" Lilly said as she paused at catch her breath, Amanda stopped and turned smiling sheepishly "Sorry, he hasn't changed he's still an arrogant bully who thinks he can just run people over as he sees fit, I won't take it" she said as she stamped her foot," Lilly saw Cooper out of the corner of her eye as he made his way to the gardens with a tray, she smiled as she said" Miss perhaps a walk in the gardens is just what you need, it'll get your mind off the Massas, "Maybe you're right Lilly, see I told you you'd be a good companion and you were worried" Amanda said as she turned towards the gardens.

Lilly led the way to the gardens, they were exquisite, all abloom with color and life as they entered through the wooden gate into a high flowering hedge, roses bloomed in every shade to the right near the hedge maze sat a bench, on the bench sat a tray of lemonade and oatmeal raisin cookies, Lilly walked over pouring a glass of lemonade and handing it to Amanda who accepted it with a smile, she took a sip her mind started to wander thinking about the man in the black coat, she walked about thinking his eyes are so blue and warm like looking into the sea on a warm day, she wondered if she should ask Lilly, she bit her lip then took a deep breath saying in her most conversational way "Lilly when I arrived a man carried my trunks up to my rooms and I just was wondering who he was um I'd like to thank him," Lilly blinked in surprise "Oh that was probably Cooper the butler he's my brother" Lilly said with pride, "Oh" she said trying not to sound disappointed, he's a slave she thought, but he's so good looking and those blue eyes and he's quite fair skinned like coffee and cream, she turned towards the maze "Well I just wanted to thank him for his assistance, she tamped down that disappointment and tried to squelch the attraction she felt, but she thought may be Lilly could see what she was feeling she'd always been told she had a glass face.

As they walked the maze, Amanda lost in thought as she thought about Cooper stood in the kitchen, looking out the window into the gardens he smiled as he saw the two women, he watched Amanda's bonneted head fascinated by her.

The sun was low in the sky as Lilly looked into the sun "Wes' better get you dressed for dinner or the Massas' will be throwing fits" Lilly said, Amanda nodded and they left the garden through the gate.

As she dressed for dinner she continued to think about Cooper as Lilly helped her into the sea green dress, it shimmered with beadwork, Lilly looked at her as Amanda stared out the window with a far-away look on her face "Miss Amanda, where did you go you're so far away" Lilly said concerned, she touched Amanda's arm, Amanda jumped startled her green eyes widened in shock, she looked at Lilly blinking like a sun blind owl "What is something wrong?" Amanda asked confused, "Miss Amanda you were a million miles away are you alright?" Lilly inquired, "I'm fine Lilly I was just thinking of my Father, he died recently and I don't feel right about marrying at this time and I really don't want to marry Mervin anyway, do I sound like a bad person" Amanda said as she bit her lip concerned looking into the mirror on the dressing table, "So you don't want to marry Massa Mervin, then why did you come?" Lilly asked, Amanda closed her eyes letting out a breath "My Mother wants me to marry him" Amanda said with dislike, Lilly nodded as she set the brush down pulling Amanda's hair into an upswept do, she put pins in Amanda's long blond hair, she stepped back eyeing her handy work.

Amanda slid the gold earbobs into her ears as Lilly layer the gold locket around Amanda's slender neck, she smiled as she looked at her reflection, it was then that she wondered if Cooper would be there.

She stood determined to ignore Mervin's lustful advances and try to get through dinner with as much grace as possible.

Cooper straightened his neck cloth as he looked in the small old mirror, he shifted his broad shoulders under the black coat he studied himself looking from side to side, he'd hoped against hope that the beautiful Amanda would notice him, the thought he'd die happy if she would smile at him, he shook his head thinking he shouldn't be thinking these thoughts there was nothing for him, but misery if he touched the new Big missy, but what he'd heard earlier haunted him so he knew that he must help her even if it cost him his life he couldn't allow another person to suffer yes he thought he'd have to keep them apart. He left the sparse cell that he shared with seventy other slaves, it was drafty and cold in the winter and sweltering in the summer, but it was all he'd ever known, he remembered as a child learning to walk on these very wooden floors, he smiled at the memory of his beautiful quiet mother he missed her terribly, but he was glad that his father was still alive and he knew he talk to Big Zeke and he would listen.

After dinner, but before dessert was served Amanda sat in the parlor with a cup of tea, Mervin paced the polished floor with a glass of whisky in this hand, Lilly stood outside the parlor, she leaned against the wall, Cooper walked into the hallway, he turned seeing her he touched her face affectionately smiling "Do you like the new Big missy?" Cooper asked, "She doesn't want to be the Big missy, I like her she's sweet, but sad she keeps to herself a lot" Lilly said wistfully "The Massas' are planning to take her money and hurt her, she likes you I can tell, Lil don't you want to help her?" Cooper said concerned,

Lilly looked at her bare feet embarrassed, she nodded "I do like her, she's good people, I'll help anyway I can" "Good" Cooper said his eyes bright with excitement and hope.

Cooper patted her shoulder as he walked towards the kitchen to get dessert.

As he entered the dining room, he set down the chocolate cake, slicing the cake he put the plates where the three people had sat, he looked at her napkin seeing it crumpled on the table knowing that her sweet full mouth had been pressed against the napkin he closed his eyes trying to down the attraction he felt.

He stood in the doorway tall and stately "his full rich voice saying "Dessert is served in the dining room" Amanda looked up seeing his features devoid of expression she felt depressed she liked the light in his eyes and his smiles, she calmed her own features before anyone could notice, McClure stood then Mervin walked over to Amanda offering her his arm she hesitated before taking it.

As they reached the dining room, Mervin held out a chair and sat down murmuring thank you she looked up finding herself staring into Cooper's' blue eyes as he poured more tea into her cup she smiled shyly unable to speak and he nodded slightly, Mervin frowned turning purple with anger "More whisky" he growled Cooper took the decanter off the side board setting it in front of Mervin, he stepped back standing by the wall, Amanda kept her head down hoping that no one could see the blush creeping up her cheeks, she'd spoken to him before why couldn't she now she thought she wanted him to know that she didn't see him as a servant, she felt so stupid she could've said thank you, she just smiled at him, "Amanda aren't you feeling well my dear?" McClure said, Amanda jerked her head up surprised "Oh I'm just fine Cousin Jonathan, just thinking long thoughts you know" she smiled sheepishly, Mervin's' smallish blue eyes narrowed suspiciously as he looked from her to Cooper, he snorted his disapproval and Amanda sighed uncomfortably as she stared at her hands.

As dinner ended Cooper came around with a tray taking plates as he came to collect Amanda's she said quietly "Thank you and thank you for the tea" "You're most welcome Miss" Cooper said with a smile was warm and sensuous, "Please call me Amanda" she said sweetly, "The HELL he will Amanda, he's slave" Mervin said annoyed, "Well in Pittsburgh, as in the rest of the North we don't have slaves people work for wages" Amanda said passionately, Cooper looked from Amanda to Mervin frightened he backed up, McClure stood up moving like a cat in spite of his limp, he stood behind Cooper who was backing towards the door, Cooper bumped into McClure, he turned suddenly, Cooper swallowed hard looking down he tugged his cropped brown hair as he stammered "I'm sorry Massa I didn't see you there" "Of course not Cooper, but you see OUR Amanda is from the North and she doesn't understand our ways so we have to educate her don't we Cooper" McClure said calmly, Cooper closed his eyes taking a deep breath, he opened his them just in time to see McClure's fist as it drove into his stomach, the blow sent him reeling to the floor where he opened and closed his mouth like a fish, as he felt the pain start to recede he moved to an elbow breathing normally.

Amanda screamed as she saw Cooper go down and tried to run to his side, but Mervin held her arm tight as she tried to jerk her free, Cooper stood suddenly keeping an arm around his middle breathing hard, Amanda bit her lip till she tasted blood, Lilly who was standing in the hallway peeked around the corner when she'd heard Amanda scream she gasped, McClure hit him again this time in the face bloodying his nose and splitting his lip, Amanda finally twisted free of Mervin's grasp running to Cooper's side "You monster" she whispered coldly she wrenched the handkerchief out of her bosom putting it to Cooper's nose, Lilly snuck into the room quietly clinging to the walls till she got to the table then she ran towards her brother, but before she could get to him McClure reached out a hand grabbing her hair, she cried out in pain he grabbed her around the waist with the other hand dropping his cane as he messaged her breast, she tried to move away but he entwined his hand tighter in her long curly hair he seized her face kissing her bruisingly as she struggled to get away, Cooper stood up saying obediently "Massa please let my sister go please" McClure suddenly let Lilly go she staggered two steps sobbing Cooper walked over hugging her close as she sobbed, they turned walking from the room, Amanda glared at McClure as she left the room.

Lilly sat on the cotton filled mattress her sobs had subsided to snuffles Cooper paced the wooden floor like a caged tiger, he had stripped off his cravat and coat "I'm going to kill him" Cooper raged "Don't say that Coop, you know what will happen, they'll lynch you and you know it" Lilly cried Cooper nodded reluctantly "What can we do" Cooper said agitated, he ran a hand through his cropped brown hair, Lilly stood wiping her hands on her homespun dress then she walked to the door "Lilly where are you going" Cooper said astonished "Miss Amanda may need me after what happened I need to tell her that I'm fine that she needn't worry" Lilly said surprisingly calm, then she walked out the door.

Amanda sat in the overstuffed mulberry colored chair she gripped the arms of the chair hard her knuckles white and a look of dread on her face, Mervin stood behind her frowning, Jonathan McClure sat behind the oak desk calmly smoking a cigar, "Amanda, you forced my hand earlier, what did you think you were going to prove, their slaves their simple they're supposed to work for us you aren't supposed to encourage them try to be equal to us" McClure said coolly, Amanda opened her mouth closing it stunned "I........I......I just wanted to thank him and show him some kindness and maybe be his friend that's all, I don't understand any of this slavery and cruelty I just don't understand" she cried shaking, Mervin looked at his father skeptically McClure looked back at Mervin doubtfully, Amanda stood wiping her sweaty hands on her gown "Well I think I'll go to my room now I'm rather tired it's been a long day, thank you for the delicious meal" Amanda said fully composed as she left the room walking slowly and purposefully to her rooms.

Amanda opened the door seeing Lilly fixing a small pallet for herself in the sitting room "The Massa told me to see to your needs, I hope you don't mind Miss Amanda" Lilly said shyly, Amanda smiled "Of course Lilly, I'm glad you're here, are you alright" she said as she hugged Lilly in true friendship and sisterhood.

The two women sat up talking most of the night, Lilly smiled as she told Amanda about her Mother Betty "She was a kitchen girl like I am, but she was also the Massa's favorite and she got certain privileges like she got to choose who she married and she married my father Big Zeek" Amanda smiled dreamily as she sipped her tea "Is she still alive your mother?" Amanda asked "No she died giving birth to me, that's what Cooper said anyway of course he was just a child himself so I don't know how much he remembers" Lilly said sadly, Amanda set her cup down, she picked up the pot while Lilly wiped her eyes, she poured more tea into Lilly's cup Lilly looked at her surprised "I should've done that you shouldn't be doing that Miss Amanda" Lilly said "Oh posh Lilly and please call me Amanda" she said "Are you sure Amanda?" Lilly said swallowing hard Amanda nodded smiling "You're my friend my almost sister" Amanda yawned widely trying to cover her mouth in time, "We should get you to bed Amanda" Lilly said as she stood up gathering up the tray she took it down to the kitchen, then she went back upstairs to help Amanda get ready for bed.

As the sun rose Cooper buttoned his coat smoothing away all the wrinkles, he closed his eyes remembering the dream Amanda was in his arms kissing him and smiling her sweet smile, he scrubbed a hand over his face knowing he had to stop this she was going to be the Big missy here he couldn't afford to be lusting after her forever he knew he had to stop feeling what he did for her, but before he did stop he needed to see her smile at him one more time, he left the room heading for the kitchens to give Della a hand, he set the table with the fine white and gold china, he set the biscuits on the side board then went back for the eggs and sausages.

Amanda rose stretching and yawning she pulled back the covers breathing in the wonderful smells from the kitchens her stomach growled, Lilly chuckled as she moved about the room, she turned seeing Amanda "what would you be wearing today" she said cheerily "I was thinking the cream colored day dress what do you think" Amanda said Lilly walked into the closet taking the dress off the rack she brought it out holding it up for Amanda to inspect, she eyed the dress thoughtfully "Hm maybe not, maybe the pink day dress" Lilly took the cream colored day dress back taking down the pink day dress and bringing it her for inspection, Amanda nodded approvingly "That's the one thank you Lilly, do you think Cooper will like this dress" Lilly giggled "You really do like my brother don't you" Amanda blushed nodding "Please don't say anything I'm not even sure he likes me, do you think he likes me Lilly?" said biting her lip, "I know my brother he likes you alright" Lilly smiled "Come on let's get you fixed up so my brother can see you in that pretty dress" Lilly said pulling her gently along.

Amanda reached the last step she looked around her green eyes catching sight of Cooper her eyes grew bright as she barely blinked she just couldn't stop watching him, Mervin strolled passed stopping in her view she blinked abruptly grinning sheepishly he held out his arm she took it reluctantly as he led her to the table pulling out her chair, she sat down staring down at her hands as Mervin frowned at her, he slid a hand threw his untidy mass of brown hair as he looked at his father with an unsettled look, McClure frowned back shaking his head slightly, annoyed, Cooper came around with the tea pot "Tea Miss" he inquired "Yes please thank you Cooper" Amanda said trying not to look at him, "So my dear what are your plans for today?" McClure asked folding his hands and resting his whiskered chin there, Amanda looked at him surprised "I don't know I hadn't really thought about it, if you have stables I'd like to go for a ride" she said as she dropped a sugar cube into her tea, "Of course my dear we have many riding horses I'll arrange it" McClure said genially, Della bustled in with a tray of sausages and rolls, Cooper walked in carrying a large tray of scrambled eggs he set it on the sideboard then he turned saying "Breakfast is served," then he bowed moving to stand by the wall, they got up to fix their plates Amanda moved passed Cooper in a swirl of pink skirts she turned her head staring at him her cheeks as rosy pink as her dress she tilted her heart shaped head smiling then she looked at the McClure's biting strawberry red bottom lip, she scurried off to join the others who were sitting down with their plates of food, after they ate Amanda returned to her rooms to change into her riding habit, Lilly stood behind her the green riding habit layer over her arm as Amanda wiggled out of the pink dress she dropped on the floor, Lilly bent to pick it up she handed the riding habit to Amanda who stepped into it buttoning the tiny pearl buttons, then Lilly set the tall black hat with the green ribbon on Amanda's snooded blond hair pinning it to her head she turned looking at her reflection in the mirror satisfied she smiled at Lilly as she left the room.

The stables were warm and dark Amanda breathed in the smell of hay and animals McClure and the groom Toby walked down the row of horses till they found the one that they thought she could handle, she mounted Arabella, the ginger colored mare snorted stamping restlessly, she snapped the reins and the horse started off like a shot when she kicked Arabella in the ribs, she laughed feeling free for the first time since her father died.

Toby followed behind her in the donkey cart as Amanda kicked the horse to a gallop she laughed feeling so free, she slowed the horse as they entered the orchard the white blossoms in full bloom, she breathed in their sweet scent as she rode through, a slight breeze blew sending petals raining down she turned her face skyward feeling the soft blossoms caress her face she closed her eyes thinking of Cooper would he touch like that, she bit her lip pushing the thought away, she rode on through the orchard to the woods beyond, the woods felt warm and safe like being in the womb, the smell of pine was thick in the air, she liked the peacefulness of this place she decided to come here again.

As she left the forest she felt better like she could take on the world, Toby waited in the donkey cart "Are you enjoying yourself Miss?" Toby said with a smile, Amanda smiled back "Oh yes, it's so pretty and peaceful here" "Yes ma'am" Toby nodded as she mounted the horse riding off back to the stables, she hoped to be able to stay away from Mervin a little longer.

She stood in the yard staring at the fields watching the slaves in the fields, she listened to them sing, they sang about hope and freedom and the more she listened the more it broke her heart, she walked around till she came to two men working on the cotton gin, one of the men stood up he took his straw hat off scratching his bald head, as he grabbed the wrench handing it to the man lying under the cotton gin, she walked over saying "Hello" "Mornin' Miss somethin' we can help you with" the tall man said "No thank you sir I'm just looking around" the tall man laughed "Sir, sir Moe did you hear that the lady just called me sir" Amanda blushed, she opened and closed her mouth not knowing what to say, Moe wiggled out from under the cotton gin smiling, the two men could be almost interchangeable the same height and bulk the same bald head and the same jovial smile on their faces, "I'm Amanda I'm so please to meet you" "Zeek and this is my son Moe glad to meet you Miss" "Oh I'm very good friends with your daughter Lilly she's a wonderful person she's been such a good friend to me" Amanda said excitedly "She's a good girl our Lilly is, I'm so glad she's become your friend Miss you seem like a good person Miss" Zeek said amiably "Would you like us to show you around the cotton shed Miss" Moe asked "Thank you Moe I'd be pleased to see the cotton shed" Amanda said kindly as she lifted the skirts of her green riding habit walking into the cotton shed, they showed her all the equipment, Amanda said conversationally "Zeek did Lilly or Cooper tell you what my Cousin Jonathan did to Lilly?" Zeek and Moe nodded "He frightened her so bad, she seems fine now, but I think she's still upset, I was so scared myself Zeek" Zeek nodded, a shadow crossed the doorway, they turned seeing Mervin standing in the doorway, he frowned as he saw Amanda with Moe and Zeek he narrowed his smallish blue eyes viciously "Amanda there you are Toby said you'd left after your ride and I didn't know where you went, come with me to the house now I'm sure you'd like to rest now" Mervin held out an arm for her to take "Thank you Zeek thank you Moe, I really enjoyed the tour thank you" she left with Mervin, they walked gracefully towards the house she with her head down biting her lip, her heart breaking for the people held in bondage to her cousin's.

Amanda ran upstairs to change out of her riding habit, Lilly stood up as she entered pulling the pins from her hair she frowned tossing the hat on the overstuffed red settee, she shook her head irritably "Mervin he's impossible Lilly absolutely impossible I can't go anywhere or do anything without him sniffing after me, oh I met your Father and your brother Moe their very nice men" Amanda said angrily, but she was slowly calming down, she took a deep breath sitting down putting her head in her hands trying not to cry Lilly walked over putting a hand on her shoulder Amanda reached for her hand squeezing as she brushed away a tear, "Well we best get you ready now Amanda come on get up paste a smile on your face and pretend to want to be with them we'll find a way to get you out of this marriage" Lilly said calmly as she pulled a sluggish Amanda to her feet, she unbuttoned the jacket of her riding habit sliding it off her shoulders to reveal the short white blouse beneath, she unbuttoned the skirt and it swished to the polished white marble floor she stepped out of it, Lilly bent to pick up the discarded clothing "What dress do you think Amanda?" she asked "Hm maybe the blue gingham with the wide collar, that should keep Mervin away from my bosom don't you think" Amanda said with a smug smile, Lilly walked out of the closet with the blue gingham dress she held it up for Amanda to inspect, Amanda nodded, Lilly helped Amanda into the dress buttoning it up the back, she turned smoothing the dress down she patted at her hair as she stared into the mirror, she straightened up smiling at Lilly who smiled as she bustled into the other room, Amanda left the room taking a deep breath she started down the stairs into the parlor, Mervin stood by the unlit fireplace a cup coffee in his hand, Jonathan McClure sat in the dark blue overstuffed chair a cup of coffee in his hand, he reached into his coat pocket removing a small silver flask he dumped a large amount of brandy into the coffee, Amanda raised her eyebrows and McClure winked as he took a sip, "Did you enjoy your ride Amanda" Mervin said irritably Amanda swallowed composing herself "As a matter of fact I did thank you Mervin" he turned taking a swallow of the coffee "What were you doing in the cotton shed and with Zeek and Moe" Mervin said his annoyance growing "Well after my ride I was walking around the yard when I saw Zeek and Moe working on the cotton gin so I went over to talk to them and they wanted to show me around so I thought why not they seemed like nice people I don't understand what's wrong?" Amanda said looking scared "Their slaves Amanda their of low morals, they'd like nothing better than to hurt you, we've had riots they were on neighboring plantations, but riot none the less where white women were taken and raped, they don't care about you we have to keep them in line" Mervin said his anger evident, Amanda stared at her hands looking frightened "I didn't know" she whispered, "Of course you didn't know you're a northerner slavery doesn't exist in the North anymore you have to trust us Amanda" Mervin said as he started to calm down, McClure stood up he leaned heavily on his cane as he walked over sitting down next to Amanda patting her hand "Trust us we have your best interests at heart you wouldn't want us to have to write to your Mother telling her that you were murdered by slaves that would kill her, your Father's' death was very hard on her as it was on you so please my dear trust us" McClure said gently, Amanda nodded slowly still staring at her hands, "Well let's get you a cup of tea my dear that will do wonders for you alright" she nodded McClure reached for the bell pull, pulling it, Cooper appeared in the doorway "Tea Cooper" McClure said, Cooper nodded walking away to get the tea, "Well I was thinking my dear of showing you off to our neighbors won't they be jealous, I thought a cotillion would be just the thing" McClure said with a smile, Amanda forced herself to smile hoping it looked genuine, McClure stood up walking out of the room to the kitchens with the menu for the evening meal, Lilly stood at the counter washing beans, "Where's Della Lilly?" McClure leisurely Lilly turned curtsying "I don't know Massa" she stammered "Shall I go find her" Lilly asked anxious to leave McClure stepped closer "Why are you so nervous Lilly, do I frighten you?" he chuckled "N....N.... No Massa" Lilly said hesitantly McClure sauntered closer patting her on the bottom slowly, Lilly gasped moving away McClure grabbed her arm pulling her closer, he uncurled her fist as he placed her palm to his groin rubbing up and down "No Massa don't do that" Lilly squealed as she tried to pull away, he dropped her hand suddenly as he heard Della singing as she walked towards the kitchens, McClure stepped back as Della entered the kitchen "Massa what can I do for you?" Della said cheerily "I wanted to discuss the dinner menu with you" McClure said as he led the way to the table.

Cooper entered the kitchens seeing the Massa, Della and Lilly, Lilly stood at the counter snapping beans, Cooper walked to the stove pouring the boiling water into the teapot, he took the jar of tea off of the shelf dumping two ladlefuls into the boiling water, then he placed the pot on the tray with cream, sugar and cookies, then he took the tray into the parlor, placing it on the table he looked at Amanda asking "Shall I pour for you Miss" she nodded slowly, he poured the sweet rich smelling tea.

Mervin stared at Cooper as he poured the tea, he narrowed his eyes moving away from the wall, and Cooper straightened up he left the room quietly.

Amanda quietly sipped her tea as Mervin moved around the room "What is it about him Amanda can you tell me, you're fascinated by him aren't you?" Mervin inquired Amanda gaped at him "Lilly is my friend and Cooper is her brother and she cares about him so I thought I could make friends with him as well" Amanda said innocently, "My Father is planning to announce our engagement at the cotillion" Mervin said conversationally Amanda looked at him with a raised eyebrow "the way I remember it being said is that if I want to marry you I will, but if I don't I'll visit then go home to Pittsburgh, I won't be forced into a marriage" Amanda said feeling backed into a corner, "You tease" Mervin exclaimed angrily, Amanda looked taken aback she blinked rapidly shocked, she stood moving towards the door, Mervin sauntered over grabbing her arm he pulled her to him kissing her bruisingly, she fought to get away, she lashed out kicking him in the shins, she moved away running out the door and up the stairs to her rooms.

CHAPTER TWO

She stood at the wash stand damp wash cloth in hand, she rubbed the cloth over her mouth she shivered discussed as she tried to wipe away the memory of his kiss, she knew she had to get away or she'd be forced into a marriage she didn't want she had to think and find a way to stop this horrible marriage from happening, the cotillion was being planned for tomorrow night she wondered if they would miss her if she just ran into the woods never to be seen or heard from again, she knew that Lilly was busy with her kitchen duties, but she was sure that if she asked her she would help her leave maybe they'd like to come with her they could start over again somewhere else, as she stood thinking Lilly bustled in with her cream colored dress laid over her arm "Amanda, I've pressed your gown that the Massa's said that they wanted you to wear tomorrow night" Lilly said Amanda's mouth opened and closed shocked "They went through my belongings" Amanda said astonished "Oh no they asked me if you had a ball gown and I said oh yes Massa its cream colored so they told me to press it so I did, I hung it in your closet" she moved to the other room to hang the dress in the closet, Amanda walked into the bedroom "Lilly if I asked for your help would you help me?" she asked nervously as she twisted lace on her

29

bodice Lilly looked at her in surprise "Well yes I'd help you if I could, what can I be doing for you" she asked "Well I was thinking I don't want to marry Mervin as you know, but they are going to force me so I thought that if I left I could start over somewhere else, so will you help me Lilly" she implored, Lilly blinked surprised she scratched the crown of her dark head the red bandana moving to and fro as she thought, "I don't see how you can sneak away, but slaves have done it so I know it's possible" she said quietly "But don't tell anyone what your planning because you never know who you can trust" Lilly said as she touched Amanda's shoulder.

The ballroom was swept out and dusted and the wooden floor was polished to a high shine, new candle sticks were set in the holders, a slave girl in a gray dress stood on a ladder polishing the wooden carvings on the wall, while another girl stood below polishing the carvings from floor level.

Della bustled around the kitchen making sure all the delicacies that would be served at the cotillion, the Massa's asked for six courses plus appetizers to be passed around by kitchen slaves in black coats and gray dresses, it promised to be quite an affair she thought she hoped the new Big missy would be pleased, she pulled the tart shells from the oven the sugared mixed berries sat in a dish on the counter to be spooned into the cooled tart shells, then she would cook the chicken for dinner, she hoped Rhea or Lilly would be in soon to help her she was becoming overwhelmed with not only dinner plans, but with food plans for the cotillion, she wiped her forehead with a cloth it was hot in the kitchen she looked out the open window wishing for a cool breeze.

Rhea walked in potatoes tied into her apron, "What took you so long girl" Della chided her "I'm sorry Della Moe asked me a question" Rhea said quietly Della raised a graying eyebrow "So it's Moe now what happened to Cooper?" Della asked interested "He don't look at me I always thought Moe was good lookin' I mean not like Cooper, but good lookin' none the less", Rhea turned to start washing and peeling the potatoes for tonight's dinner.

Cooper inspected all uniforms that the other slaves would be wearing tomorrow, making sure that each one was perfectly maintained, he wondered if Amanda could dance he imagined that she'd glide across the floor like an angel, he wished he'd be able to dance with her, knew he'd never be able to he didn't know why he was torturing himself he had to stop he thought as he finished his inspection, then he went to inspect the good silver.

As Cooper entered the kitchens, he walked to the drawer pulling it out he, he laid a cloth down, and he picked up each piece looking at it closely from all directions setting them down.

Mervin strolled into the ballroom he slid the French doors closed the two slave girls turned looking scared, he stood with one eyebrow raised, the girls slowly walked forward curtseying "Hello Massa" they said in unison, "Belle, I want you to come to my room this evening and Constance I want you to come tomorrow" Mervin said lustfully he spun on a heel opening the doors and walking through, he grinned rubbing his hands together, he decided that he would pretend that they were Amanda till he could have her in his bed for real.

Amanda and Lilly walked out the door strolling towards the gardens, Amanda stared into the kitchens, she watched

Cooper move around the kitchen, she wished she could be close to him to talk to him, she wondered about him he seemed so mysterious, maybe she could get Lilly and Cooper to come with her when she ran away.

They strolled around the gardens, "What do you think of my idea I mean to leave" she asked Lilly watched her "I think it's a good idea, Cooper told me that he overheard the Massa's talking about taking your money and that Massa Mervin just wants to bed you" Lilly said sincerely "Well I knew about Mervin, but to take my father's money is not right, I mean to say that I'm not greedy it's just that he left it to me for my use" Amanda said concerned she took a deep breath "Well I'm not going to get trapped in a marriage not of my choosing, I'm going to find a way to get out of it" she said stubbornly, she looked out across the gardens to the cotton fields seeing the slaves laboring in the hot Virginia sun, how she wished she could help them all, but she couldn't even seem to help herself, she had to find a way she thought, she turned walking through the maze, she kept her face turned away afraid that Lilly would see her tears, Lilly walked behind her, her brow furrowed "Amanda are you alright did I upset you by telling you" Lilly asked "No, I'm just thinking, I'm fine" she said as she turned a corner and finding a wall of shrubbery she walked on through the maze, the was high in the sky as Cooper stepped into the gardens, he looked resplendent in his black coat, creased black pants and polished black shoes, but the bright white shirt looked great against his lightly tanned skin Amanda swallowed hard blinking like she was staring into the sun "Luncheon is served" he said gazing directly at Amanda as he spoke, she moved passed him lightly touching his arm saying "Thank you Cooper" she said sweetly as she left the gardens, he smiled breathing deeply he walked from the gardens opening the door for the two women.

Amanda sat down at the table, Cooper set the salad in front her he let his pinkie finger slid across her hand as he set the plate in front of her, she smiled at him she hoped it looked like a smile of thanks, he shifted the tray around as he walked over to the McClure's to give them their salads, he walked away to give them the soup that Della was dishing out, he came into the kitchen as Della was wiping her sweating brow with a handkerchief that she kept in the bosom of her dress, he set the tray down, she set each bowl onto the tray as she filled them, he smelled the rich smell of tomato basil soup, he lifted the tray walking out into the dining room for Amanda and the Massas to eat.

Cooper cleared the salad and soup dishes taking them to the kitchen, he set the tray down as Della cut the deep dish apple pie placing the pie on plates, Cooper hoisted the tray taking it out to the dining room, he sat a slice of pie in front of Amanda who thanked him as she picked up her fork, he moved over to where the McClure sat to give them their pie.

Rhea set to work on the dishes, Cooper walked into the kitchen with the last of the dishes, he set the tray down touching Della on the cheek as she dished out the soup for the house slaves to eat, and he sat down at the kitchen table to eat his soup and sandwich.

Amanda stood in the Library, she searched the shelves for a good book to read, Mervin stood in the doorway he licked his fleshy lips greedily as he stepped forward, he grabbed her around the waist, she screamed in shock as she ran into his chest, she pushed at his ill-fitting brown coat as he kissed her bruisingly he opened her mouth with his thumb and forefinger on either side of her face he thrust his tongue into her mouth as she squealed in protest of the assault, she kicked him in the shins moving swiftly away, she ran around the other side of the chair he moved shoving the chair aside she ran to the fireplace taking a poker from the rack that stood alongside a basket of wood she brandished it like a sword her breathing labored as she said angrily "Don't ever do that again, don't you ever touch me again" she moved slowly passed never taking her eyes off of him, as she reached the doorway she tossed the poker onto the floor she turned running from the room, as she hit the stairs she ran into Cooper who was taking the stairs two at a time his blue eyes wide with fear as he said "I heard someone scream" she put a hand to her chest breathing hard she swallowed audibly saying near tears "He attacked me, Mervin attacked me please keep him away from me" he nodded putting a hand on her back he guided her upstairs saying "I'll send Lilly to you, you go to your rooms and lock the doors, I'll tell her to knock" she nodded then she turned lifting her skirts she ran up the steps to her rooms she locked the door tight, she leaned against the door sighing with relief, she moved to the mulberry overstuffed chair, she curled her legs underneath her, when she heard the knock at the door she stood up going to the door she unlocked it and opened it Lilly walked in with a loaded tray, she set the tray on the small table by the chair she bent taking the pot of tea and a cup off the tray she poured the tea handing it to Amanda who accepted it with a smile she picked up the spoon and the sugar bowl, they sipped their tea Amanda breathed in the rich sweet aroma, she looked up as Lilly took the flask out of her pocket dumping a good dollop into Amanda's' tea, she then handed Amanda a plate from the tray, she bit into the ham sandwich savoring the taste they talked the rest of the day.

Jonathan McClure sat in his study looking over his books when Rhea walked in, she curtseyed saying quietly "Afternoon Massa I's just come with the dinner menu Della says she's real busy and can't get away" she walked up to the desk laying it over the papers already there, McClure leaned back in the chair rubbing his knee he winced in pain the injury was still so painful, but he knew ways of dealing with the pain, "Rhea would you help me with something?" he asked trying to sound kind "If I can Massa" she said unsure "Come over here and rub my knee the injury is still so painful" he said she knelt down in front of him her small hands went to his left knee rubbing in a circular motion, he relaxed into the massage, looking down at her noticing her bent head, he watched her breasts rise and fall with each breath she took he grinned savagely leaning forward just a bit moving his hand ever so slowly he reached into her bodice squeezing her breasts she jumped up squealing, she fell back against the desk where he grabbed her around the waist pulling her towards him, once she was on his knee, she continued to struggle till she got away. She ran from the room crying, her heart pounded in her chest. The massas' could be so cruel, scaring and upsetting the slaves that worked for them. She walked down the hall wiping her face on her sleeve, he'd scared her bad this time. McClure grinned as he sat at his desk he picked up the menu looking it over.

He looked at the door, shaking his head, he thought the little chit would be more cooperative.

Rhea ran into the kitchens and out the door running down the path to her mother's quarters, she opened the door seeing all the children happily playing on the floor with cornhusk dolls and crudely made tops "Mama" she said quietly "I need to talk to you could we step outside" Esther put her mending down she stood up with a crackle of old bones they walked out the door, they stood on the ramshackle porch Rheas' arms were folded under her breasts, she bit her lip trying not to cry as she said " He did it again Mama the Massa scared me so bad Mama, he tried to hit me can I wash up here before I return to work" Esther looked down at her gnarled hands she painfully clenched them tight saying "I'm so sorry child" she blinked back the tears she saw in her daughter's eyes, Esther opened her arms and Rhea stepped inside feeling safe in an unsure world.

Lilly helped Amanda dress for dinner, she sat down in front of the mirror as Lilly brushed her long blond hair, she took the pins sweeping her hair into chiffon do, she stared at the result approvingly wishing that she was dressing for Cooper, she stood up smiling "Thank you Lilly" she said brushing down the front of her dress she swirled around walking to the door she griped knob tightly breathing deep she pulled open the door walking through, she walked down the stairs into the dining room, the amber and cream silk gown shimmered in the firelight, Cooper pulled out her chair she sat down saying "Thank you" he smiled he was hoping the look said you're welcome, Cooper came into the dining room the tray laden with plates of baked chicken, mashed potatoes and string beans, as they ate Amanda refused to look at Mervin who continued to stare at her, he frowned stuffing a large spoonful of mashed potatoes into his mouth as he noticed her gazing at Cooper again.

McClure raised a graying eyebrow as he noticed which direction she was looking, he had to keep them apart he'd warn Cooper he thought maybe even threaten to flog him, yes that would work he thought as he sliced into a piece of chicken folding it into his mouth he chewed and swallowed, out of the corner of his eye he saw Lilly edge along the wall to where Cooper stood, they spoke briefly and she disappeared into the hall, he watched Lilly move thinking about the kiss, Rhea was getting boring he needed fresher game Lilly was just the thing he needed to get his mind off his troubles.

Amanda walked gracefully up the stairs she was so glad supper had ended, she couldn't stand to be around Mervin a second longer, she turned around seeing Lilly behind her she felt better, looking over Lilly's head she saw Cooper walk down the hall a pile of linens laying over his arms as he made his way to the laundry, she watched his retreating back it was ramrod straight.

Amanda sat in front of the mirror pulling pins from her blond hair, Lilly stood behind her brush in hand, she ran a hand through her hair trying to feel if all the pins were gone, Lilly moved forward sliding the brush through Amanda's hair, she braided it tying the pink ribbon around the tail end, Amanda stood Lilly unbuttoned the dress stepping out, Lilly picked up the dress folding it over her arm she walked to the closet hanging it up she took down the white robe and nightgown taking it over to where Amanda sat removing her jewelry, she turned away from the mirror and from Lilly as she removed her shift laying it on the bench, Lilly slipped the nightgown over her head then she wrapped the robe around her shoulders, Amanda slipped her arms into the sleeves, she went to the open window breathing in the warm scented air, she could faintly hear the sounds of singing, she closed her eyes trying to relax "Is there anything I can get for you Amanda?" she asked worried "No, no thank you I just want to forget about Mervin and what he did" she said still feeling the urge to go and wash, "Don't worry about me Lilly I'm fine I just want to forget" Amanda said blinking back tears Lilly nodded heading for the door.

Jonathan McClure stood in the doorway of his study, he called out to her as she walked passed on her way to the kitchen" Lilly could you come here and massage my leg for me it hurts so much" Lilly walked into the study she sat down on the floor wrapping her hands around his leg she rubbed at the injured leg, McClure smirked as he looked down her bodice, he moved his hand ever so slowly to her breasts she saw the hand out of the corner of her eye she jumped up shouting "No" she ran from the room into the kitchen shaking and crying, she leaned against the doorjamb trying to take deep breaths Della and Rhea turned when they heard her approach, Della bustled over with a worried look on her face "What's wrong child, are you ill?" she asked as she placed a hand on her forehead "N....n....no I'm fine Della, I just had a start I'm fine" she said with a forced smile, she turned reaching for an apron she tied it around her waist she walked over to the sink plunking in hands in a tub full dirty dishes.

Cooper leaned in the doorway a slight smile on his handsome face as he watched the women work, "The linens are in the wash room, is there anything else you need me to do?" he asked straightening, all three women looked at each other saying in unison "No" Cooper shrugged turning he headed into the Master's' study.

Cooper knocked on the door, the door was a jar, but he knocked anyway just to make sure not to upset the Master "Who is it?" came the irritated answer "It's me Massa, Cooper I was just wondering if there was anything I could get for you?" Cooper said modestly as he entered the room, it smelled of bourbon and cigar smoke wafter through the air, he wrinkled his long nose at the stench, he watched as the Massa sat in the high backed leather chair his feet up on the desk sipping from a crystal glass a lit cigar in his hand "No, I'm fine Cooper that will be all" he said absently waving a hand, Cooper nodded leaving the room as quietly as he entered it he made his way upstairs to the small corner room he stripped off his jacket and shoes and then he stood up to remove his black pants, he lay down on the cot he took a deep breath letting it out slowly before closing his eyes he put his hands behind his head enjoying the quiet of the warm evening, he let his mind wander to dinner he watched her, all her movements were so delicate and refined she would make Massa Mervin a beautiful wife, but the very thought of her with Massa Mervin made him sick, he sat up taking off his socks then he lay back down wiggling his toes as he drifted off to sleep.

Mervin belted his red silk robe, Belle stood by the fireplace, she was pressed up against the wall the line of her shoulders hunched as she tried to make herself small, she dropped to a crouch laying her head on her knees, she choked back a sob as Mervin turned towards her he laid a hand on her cheek, she cringed in fear trying to draw back, but there was nowhere to go "Come" he said as he pulled her up by her upper arms, she tried to pulled away, but she wasn't strong enough, he picked her up carrying her to the bed where he dumped her unceremoniously upon it, she tried to scramble off the edge, but Mervin grabbed her by the back of her dress throwing her back onto the bed where she landed with a thump, he covered her with himself moving against her while she whimpered and pleaded for him to stop. She fought her way free from him by scratching his face. He yelled out.

She scrambled off the bed running from the room he picked up his discarded robe, he stumbled to the mirror to see the damage to his face. She ran for the slave quarters as tears ran down her ebony cheeks, she reached her parents cabin she opened the door moving quickly through she slammed the door behind her leaning up against it, her parents looked up from their modest meal "I'm sorry" she said quietly, her Mother Doris stood up wiping her hands on her apron her brow furrowed as she came closer "Did the Massa hurt you?" she asked putting a hand on her shoulder she nodded breaking down, she pulled her closer hugging her to herself, her Father Clovis stood up he pulled his daughter to himself as he wept.

Constance moved down the hall the bundle of clean linens in her arms, she was tired she'd been scrubbing the wood work in the ballroom for what seemed like hours or years and the area between her shoulder blades hurt like blazes, but she knew that Massa Mervin wouldn't care he'd told her to come to his room tonight and she knew full well what he expected and she felt the dread in the pit of her stomach, but she knew that if she didn't go he would find her and drag her, so she resigned herself to what was to come later, she reached the dining room she took off the table cloth that was on and put on one that was so fancy that it had gold woven into it, she thought about the cotillion tomorrow maybe she could sneak a peek at the ladies in their finery, how she longed for nice things, but she knew that she would never have nice things, she sighed wiping her brow with the sleeve of her dress as she worked.

Amanda stood in front of the full length mirror in her room she brow furrowed as she tried to decide what dress to wear to the cotillion, she wanted to look nice, but she didn't want Mervin fawning over her his lustful looks were making her ill so she decided nothing low cut or he'd be looking down her bodice so it was settled on the high necked peach dress was the one she would wear, Lilly stood back she moved from side to side gaging how the dress looked and what she would do with Amanda's abundant blond hair "Hmmmm" she said thinking out loud "Maybe an upswept with some curls no ringlets hanging down" Amanda turned smiling as she nodded, she tried to sound excited, but all she felt was anxiety, she really didn't want to go to the cotillion, but she knew that she had to go.

Amanda stood on the flower covered hill overlooking the fields, she watched as the people toiled how she longed to help them to tell them there was a better way that they didn't have to live like this in poverty and ignorance. She listened to their songs as they worked, all about FREEDOM it made her sad their songs, she turned away blinking back tears, she looked up seeing Toby, the groom standing near her horse, he gently patted the cream colored gelding as he held onto the reins, she sighed walking towards the horse she put her foot in the stirrup swinging her leg up she fitted herself into the side saddle she turned as she noticed Toby move behind her horse his head down waiting for her to spur the horse on.

Amanda started up the walk, she noticed some women putting torches in the ground along the walkway, she took a deep breath feeling slightly ill, but she knew it was just nerves meeting all those people having to pretend that she wanted this marriage to Mervin, she found her mind wandering to Cooper would he be there she hoped so maybe she could get to know him, but then she thought probably not Mervin and Jonathan wouldn't leave her side not at a party such as that, she remembered how he watched her, every little move she made seemed to draw his notice, she secretly hoped that Cooper was impressed by her, she wanted to talk to him, she didn't understand why he fascinated her so, her eyes widened when she reached the bottom step only to see Cooper on the top step a rug folded in his hands, she moved aside her back against the railing "Oh no ma'am" he said quietly "You go first" she smiled "Thank You Cooper, but I think I'd like to stay out here maybe we could get to know each other a little" she said even as the blush crept up her neck into her face, he studied her his blue eyes taking in every detail, the green and white striped dress she wore, the green ribbon braided into her pale blond hair, her green eyes that sparkled like emeralds, he nodded "If you'd like, I'm just going beat the rugs if it gets to dusty for you let me know" "Oh I beat the rugs at home so I should be fine" she said cheerily as she fell into step beside him, "Have you lived here long" she asked, one brown eye brow raised in disbelief, was she joking he thought "All my life Miss Amanda ma'am" he said trying to keep the mocking tone from his voice, she stared down at her shoes thinking stupid, stupid he's going to think you're ignorant, you know he's a slave don't remind him, "Sorry" she said barely above a whisper as she raising her head, he noticed that she was biting her lower lip. The paddle came down with a whack sending dust flying in all directions, they both coughed, but Cooper continued the methodical movements as Amanda turned away her eyes burning, she turned back around clearing her throat she walked over to the bucket pulling out another paddle she took a rug off the pile hanging it over the clothesline she started her own whacks on the blue and green flowered rug, Cooper watched her intrigued she had beat rugs before he thought surprised didn't she have servants to do her work for her even the Massas' had slaves to do the work while they ran the plantation, she was to be mistress here she shouldn't be working he thought she should be sitting on the veranda a cup of tea in her lilly white hand, he pulled the rug down folding it carefully as he set it on the steps then he moved behind Amanda he took the paddle out of her hands in mid swing she turned blinking in astonishment "What??" she asked "I shouldn't have let you help me it was wrong of me" he said seriously "You need the help and I'm here and I wanted to get to know you, your sister Lilly is already a good friend why can't we be friends" or more she thought she smiled trying to cover the blush that was creeping up her neck, he wet his lips looking at her intently as he said "Miss Amanda I'm a slave and you're to be the mistress here we all know it" "Cooper I've never owned slaves I don't think it's right and if you really want to know the truth I don't want to marry Mervin he was a horrible boy and he's an even worse man" she said in a flurry of words, she sighed feeling better, Cooper's eyes widened in shock as he said "But you're here to marry Massa Mervin" she shook her head saying troubled "I know I know it was my mother's' and my cousins idea and I appear to have no say in my own life" Cooper felt a thrill of hope she didn't love Massa Mervin, he wished she could be with him oh to touch her and kiss her, to wrap his fingers in her long golden tresses, he had to stop he thought as he took the rug down that she had beaten he folded it setting it on top of the first rug he turned back to continue to beat the rugs, she frowned standing her ground she wasn't going to leave just because he didn't want her to beat rugs, she sighed audibly, he cocked his dark head towards her trying to hide the smile she wanted to be around him he thought feeling that same surge of hope could she ever want him the way he wanted her, he watched as she moved around the yard, she stood by the flower that Old Jeb had planted for Big missy Angelica before she went off to Europe to live, he'd always wondered why she left like she did, he covertly watched Miss Amanda as she bent to smell the roses, oh how he wished he were free so he could be with her, but he wasn't he turned away closing his eyes he breathed deeply before turning back around, as he turned around Amanda chose that moment to show him the most dazzling smile and he felt his breath stop in his throat, she walked over a rose in hand a small flirtatious smile played on her full wide mouth as she strolled by "Will you be at the cotillion?" she asked sweetly, he nodded saying quietly "I will be answering the door" "Oh" she said barely above a whisper, her cousin Jonathan chose that moment to come around the corner from the fields, he wiped his cane in the tall grass he grimaced at the coppery smell of blood, as he came closer he noticed Amanda standing there "Amanda just who I wanted to see" Jonathan said seriously, she swallowed thinking this can't be good, he pointed at her frowning "You forced me into that I hope your happy" he said crossly, she gaped at him as he walked by "Cousin I don't understand what are you talking about?" she asked with a twinge of fear in her voice "Mervin told me that you were in the cotton shed with two male slaves, they can be very dangerous Amanda especially with an innocent young girl such as yourself" he said gravely she swallowed "Nothing happened they were just showing me around the cotton shed, I thought if I'm going to be living here I should get to know the people here" she declared, Jonathan laughed lightly saying "Oh my dear you're such an innocent you can't trust these people I could tell you a million stories about slave riots in this part of the county, but those stories are not for your ears they would frighten you to death, come along my dear you should get ready for the cotillion it will be the most extraordinary time of your life I promise you" "Yes Cousin Jonathan" she said quietly bowing her head, several strands of blond hair escaped her tightly braided hair, she brushed them out of her face as she followed obediently behind her cousin.

Cooper turned back to the rugs, he tried not to think about Amanda as he finished.

He knew later he'll have to check on Moe and his father; he paled knowing that they'd both been flogged.

As he finished with the rugs, setting them back in their proper places on the floor, he knew he would have just enough time to see his father and brother; he'd have to hurry and get ready before the guests arrived.

Cooper started down the worn path to the slave quarters, as he opened the door; Lilly looked up her face pale and tear-stained.

"How are they?" Cooper asked concerned, he walked forward kneeling down, he placed his hands on his father and brother's shoulders "I'm so sorry Daddy, Moe what can I do for you?" his blue eyes flooding with tears "I know son" Zeeke said his gentle brown eyes glazed with pain "You best go, the Cotillion, the Massa will be upset if you're not ready" Zeeke said trying to hide his pain "I best go too Miss Amanda will need help getting ready" Lilly said as she leaned over kissing first her father's cheek then her brother's, they both stood heading for the door as an aging slave Aggie ambled into the room, she looked at Lilly and Cooper and then at Zeeke and Moe "Don't worry we'll take care of them" she said reassuringly, Cooper nodded his thanks.

They started out the door to the Big House.

As they walked Lilly stifled a sob "Daddy and Moe, Oh Lordy Cooper "Cooper pulled her into an embrace as he whispered "I know Lilly, but we have to be strong, we can't let this get to us Daddy and Moe will need our strength" he set her at arm's length as he said" Miss Amanda will need you we best get back to the Big House "she sniffled wiping her face on her apron, he rubbed her shoulders.

Lilly nodded and they walked the rest of the way to the Big House in silence.

Cooper shrugged into his crisp white shirt, he buttoned the buttons then he tied the black bow tie then he pulled on the black jacket.

He knew he had to hurry to get to the door when the guests arrive.

Amanda gracefully glided down the staircase the smell of fresh flowers and perfumes were overwhelming, she didn't know how she would stand it.

As she reached the bottom step Mervin came forward, she pasted on a smile that she hoped was convincing as she took his arm and she was led into the throng of people.

Jonathan stood by the white marble fireplace a glass whisky in his hand.

He looked up to see Amanda and Mervin as they slipped through the crowd, his face brightened as he tapped ring on his glass to get everyone's attention "Everyone thank you for coming. I have an announcement that will please you all, my son Mervin is announcing his engagement to the lovely Amanda Green of Pittsburgh, Pennsylvania "Jonathan said with a smile the crowd erupted in applause for the happy couple, Cooper could just see Amanda through the crowd, she was pale, much more than usual he thought as the musicians struck up a waltz for the couple.

Mervin twirled her around the floor as onlookers gazed at her beauty.

Cooper stood by the door, he turned away for a moment wishing he was the one dancing with Amanda, but he knew that was never to be she was to be the Big missy here and all he could do was dream about her.

He would make a vow to her tomorrow he decided to be always be there for her and to protect her.

Cooper watched his frustration growing as he watched man after man dance with her till he was told to announce dinner.

The air in the dining room was ripe with gossip as the succulent ham dinner was being eaten.

Amanda was happy to be away from Mervin and Jonathan, she was seated next to a nice elderly couple, the Scotts, and Mrs. Scott was quite chatty where Mr. Scott was quiet and thoughtful.

Mr. Scott had a beautiful ruby pin in his tie.

Amanda decided she liked the couple immediately, she hoped they would become her good friends.

Amanda noticed no one gave the slaves any recognition, they were for lack of a better word invisible, there were no thank you's as Cooper came around with a bottle of wine to fill a glass, she was shocked she always thanked the servants Da had taught her that the servants are the backbone of a household.

Poor Cooper, she thought and Lilly, dear sweet Lilly they deserve better than this, then she thought of her mother, she treated the servant the same way, she blinked in surprise at the thought that crossed her mind what if it's this southern culture that makes people needed but invisible, what must Cooper and Lilly and the other slaves what must they be thinking they can't like being treated this way.

"Did you go somewhere dear?" Mrs. Scott said, when Amanda didn't answer she cleared her throat making Amanda jump, "Sorry" she said sheepishly "My mind just wandered off, I'm so sorry Mrs. Scott" "That's alright my dear isn't it

Edgar" she nodded to her husband who nodded back as he buttered another slice of bread.

Cooper suddenly appeared again with Lilly close behind they carried trays of cookies and tarts, they placed them on the sideboard then they retreated to towards the kitchens.

Cooper appeared again with a large tea set, he set it next to the trays of sweets the he withdrew himself from the party goers company.

Mervin didn't waste much time in helping himself to the deserts.

Amanda stood up, she made her way to the sideboard to pour herself a soothing cup of tea, she knew it would help her do battle with these people and their outlooks on other people.

As dinner wore on Amanda felt more and more stifled, she had to escape, but where where could she go that they wouldn't find her.

She stood suddenly making her way out of the room on shaky legs, the gardens they might not look for her there; she lifted her skirts running as fast as she could, she collapsed on the bench breathing long unsteady breaths.

She looked up when a twig snapped to see Cooper standing there with a concerned look on his face "Miss Amanda are you alright I saw you run in here like your tail was on fire, sorry I beg your pardon for being crude Miss" he said blushing Amanda smiled reassuringly at him as she said "It's alright Cooper you did nothing wrong, I guess I did run in here that fast I needed to get away it's all happening too fast and I'm powerless to stop it I don't want this marriage" she looked at him as she blinked away tears.

He moved closer to her on the bench their knees touching, her bottom lip trembled and he touched her cheek brushing away a crystalline tear, she leaned into his hand as his thumb brushed her lips, how he wanted to kiss those ruby lips as he leaned in to do so he heard it "Step away from her Cooper NOW!!!" he jumped up as if he'd caught fire "My apologies Massa I only meant to comfort her, she's in distress" he said as true fear shot through him he swallowed hard, he turned as if to leave when Mervin said in a deadly whisper "Stay where you are" Cooper froze Mervin closed the distance between them Mervin though shorter than Cooper was bulker, Cooper had the height and a lean wiry strength, Mervin stood firm as he backhanded Cooper crossed the mouth blood pouring from his nose "YOU WILL KEEP YOUR HANDS OFF HER" Mervin shouted his face a mottled reddish "My apologies Massa" Cooper said quietly as he stared down at his feet "I meant no harm" "You never mean to harm, but you do a great deal of it, go get out of here" Mervin said still seething, Cooper started off at a run hoping that the Massa wouldn't call him back.

Mervin turned to Amanda "YOU, you keep tempting him why?" he said as he grabbed her arm jerking painfully as he pulled her against him, Amanda tried to pull away but couldn't "I---I---I didn't know that I was tempting anyone" she stammered Mervin laughed "You naive little girl You don't even know what you do to men, perhaps I should show you" he twisted her arm behind her back he pulled her more forcefully against him, she tried to wiggle away, but she couldn't move, he grabbed her face bruisingly kissing her hard "I don't know where those love birds have gone too"

CHAPTER THREE

Jonathan could be heard saying, the sounds of people talking were getting closer, Mervin suddenly released Amanda who staggered away sitting down hard, she rubbed her arm it hurt bad, but she couldn't let anyone know.

Jonathan and the Scotts rounded the corner seeing Mervin standing near the bench and Amanda perched on it Mrs. Scott chortled happily "Oh I think we might have interrupted something don't you agree Edgar I'm so happy for you sweet children starting your lives together, well come along Edgar let's leave them in peace" Amanda suddenly stood "I think I'll join you Mrs. Scott I've had enough fresh air, I think some tea is in order don't you think" she said hoping her voice didn't betray her fear.

She walked unsteadily behind the Scotts, as Mrs. Scott continued to chatter "Well I said to Edgar as you hurried away I thought you might be ill so I asked our good host about why you disappeared and you know I couldn't keep my mind off of it so I insisted that Mr. McClure find you to make sure you were alright" "I'm fin-" Amanda started to say when Mrs. Scott continued to speak "I you seem alright maybe a little nervous, but you shouldn't be it's only natural that you'd want to be with your betrothed, he's a good man I've known him since he was a little boy so shy and polite you're getting a true gentleman my dear you should be proud" Mrs. Scott patted her hand as she continued talking all the way back to the house.

Cooper sat in the kitchen at the table where Della fussed over him "Your nose boy takes more abuse child honestly Cooper what were you thinking she's to be the Big missy and you you're chasing after her like a dog after a bitch in heat" Cooper lowered his eyes she was right he knew that, but oh he couldn't seem to help himself" "Della you're right I know it there's just something about her I don't understand it I can't seem to help myself she just draws me to her, you know she doesn't want to marry Massa Mervin" Cooper said as Della continued to dab at his nose.

Suddenly the bell rang, Cooper jumped up sighing as he made his way to the dining room, and he picked up the empty trays taking them to the kitchen as the guests left the dining room for the ball room, where the dancing would resume.

Cooper took his station at the door where guests walked in and out, some guests strolled the grounds walking all the way to the gazebo on the rise in the hill overlooking the main house.

Mervin paced the floor of his room, he'd told that slut Constance that he wanted to see her, where was she? It was then that a shy rap on the door could be heard, he stalked to the door throwing it open, Constance stood there frightened and shy, she knew full well that he'd hurt her he always did "Well" Mervin said impatiently "I'm sorry Massa, Della needed help in the kitchens, I came as soon as I could, please don't be angry" she said fear sliding down and settling in her stomach to sit like a lead ball.

"Strip bitch strip" Mervin said angrily as he folded his arms over his chest.

Constance swallowed hard as she unbuttoned the black and white maid uniform, as the material slithered to the floor Mervin grabbed her pinning her hard against the wall, he unbuttoned his pants then he shoved her knees apart saying "We have to make this quick I'm due back in the ballroom" he impaled her grinding against her furiously till he was sated.

Mervin straightened his stock and tie as he rejoined the dancing in the ballroom; he searched the room for Amanda who was dancing with their neighbor Alan Stockdale who bred champion race horses, his own horse Warrior was from the Stockdale stables.

He started heading in their direction when Sally Quinn sauntered passed, she turned her head and smiled her famous come thither smile, Mervin smiled back, Sally he always liked Sally with her long black hair and her bright blue eyes she was considered the belle of the county.

It also helped that she was rather lose with her favors.

She slid her white gloved hand up his arm as she said "It's so good to see you Mervin, I heard you were getting married congratulations she's beautiful" "Thank you Sally, it's so good to see you as well how have you been?" Mervin said as he mentally striped her.

"I've been well Daddy took me into Richmond to buy the material for the dress I'm wearing tonight, do you like my dress?" Mervin grinned wolfishly as he said "Yes very much" "Have you taken you bride to be to your bed yet?" Sally asked trying not to sound jealous, there was a time she had hoped he would marry her.

"No not yet she's being difficult, she fights me when I try to kiss her" Mervin said with true frustration "You poor poor dear" Sally said as she tried not to let the grin of triumph show "So all you've been bedding is slaves?" she said interested Mervin nodded Sally smiled "Well I'm still available if you want" Sally said coyly Mervin grabbed her hand as they dashed out the door to the gazebo.

Once they reached their destination they sat for a moment to catch their breaths.

Mervin ravaged her mouth, she clutched him tightly in her arms, he slid him hand down her dress to fondle her breasts, she moaned against his mouth.

They stood as he rucked up her ruby colored skirts, he unbuttoned himself knowing that she'd be wet and wanting he slammed into her hard over and over again till he was sated.

Sally smoothed her skirts over her hips once they were done "You can do that to me anytime you want Mervin, just let me know alright" Mervin grinned "Really, Sally I'm hoping to get in-between Amanda's legs soon, till then we can be together."

Amanda sat with a group of women Mrs. Scott had introduced her to, they chatted animatedly becoming fast friends.

As the guests started to leave she hugged the new friends she had made sorry to see them go.

Mervin stood at her side as she bade farewell to Sunshine Morre a spirited red- headed beauty whose beau was Alan Stockdale she hoped that they would marry soon.

Mervin smiled at her as she started to climb the stairs "Do you need help with your dress Amanda, I'd be pleased to help you" Mervin said "Trying not to sound lustful "No thank you Mervin I'm sure I can manage, If not I'm sure Lilly will help me" she said tightly then she spun on a heel continuing up the stairs.

Cooper pulled off the last of the linens he smirked thinking he just doesn't get it, she doesn't want you Mervin, and he walked past heading towards the kitchens.

Della and several kitchen girls were in the kitchen putting things back in order, Della fanned herself with her apron as she waddled around she noticed Cooper walk past "This is the last, is there anything else Della" Cooper asked hoping he could get some sleep, Della smiled knowing just how tired he was, they were all tired "No I think that's it Cooper, go get some sleep you've earned it" Della said sweetly as she moved towards the back room where her own bed called out to her.

Cooper climbed the servants stairs heading to his own bed when he saw Amanda and Lilly on the stairs, "Cooper I just wanted to say I'm sorry for the way Mervin treated you, it was my fault I'm so sorry he hurt you, are you alright" Amanda asked concerned, he noticed that she was chewing her bottom lip, he smiled "I'm fine Miss Amanda is there anything I can get for you" he said in a true servants tone "Cooper please don't be like that" Amanda pleaded grabbing his arm, he stared at his feet then he met her eyes saying genuinely "I'm fine you needn't worry about me" she breathed a sigh of relief, she leaned in kissing him on the cheek, she turned to Lilly nodding as they walked away.

Cooper stared after them his heart pounding against his ribcage, she kissed him it was on the cheek, but she had kissed him, Amanda turned looking back, her smile mirroring his own as they both marveled at the power that is attraction.

As they entered the room Amanda was all too happy to take her shoes off, her feet were killing her, she was so glad that she'd worn the high collared peach dress that had stopped Mervin and the other men from ogling her.

Cooper, she thought that he was going to kiss her in the garden, she wondered what his kiss would be like gentle yet strong she thought like the man himself, he doesn't carry himself like a slave she thought he carried himself like royalty, his back always straight he never slouched, he walked with such grace.

She was still thinking about Cooper as she crawled into bed pulling the covers up to her chin, she snuggled down her mind ticking away as she slowly fell into a troubled but deep sleep.

Amanda rolled away from the light, the sun stinging her eyes, "Morning Miss Amanda" sang a cherry Lilly, Amanda narrowed her eyes pulling the pillow over her head she crawled deeper into the blankets "Now Miss Amanda come on now you have to get up the Massas is waitin' on you so is your breakfast" Lilly said sternly as she pulled the bed sheets down making Amanda squirm "We's do this every mornin' Miss Amanda come on ""Fine" Amanda grumbled as she leapt from the bed stretching and yawning "Oh it feels like I just went to sleep, it can't be morning already" she complained Lilly's mouth twitched "I'm afraid it is" Lilly said matter of factly as she helped Amanda wash and get dressed.

Amanda sat gracefully in the chair opposite Mervin who looked a little worse for wear, good she thought hopefully he'll leave her alone and she can put her guard down at least a little.

Cooper came around with her tea, the bruises on his face evident, Amanda inwardly cringed it was her fault he was so bruised she made up her mind she would apologize to him later, she would find him a beg his forgiveness it killed her that her own family treated people like this "Thank you Cooper" she said sweetly the corners of her mouth turning up "My pleasure miss" Cooper said quietly then he moved away pouring coffee into the men's cups.

Amanda dug into the ham and eggs as Cooper came around with fried potatoes in a bowl, "Thank you Cooper" she said meeting his eyes and seeing the same feelings there that she was feeling herself, Cooper nodded as he moved away.

"So my dear what are your plans for today" Jonathan said as he lowered his cup "Oh I thought I'd go for a ride today if you don't mind Cousin Jonathan" she said pleasantly "Of course my dear" Jonathan said kindly as he pick up a piece of toast buttering it.

She bit into her own toast which stuck in her thought and tasted like sawdust, she chewed hoping that no one saw her discomfort; she couldn't wait to be away from them.

Over the rim of her tea cup, she saw Cooper give her a knowing look; he understood her unhappiness and her discomfort her one bright spot she couldn't wait to have a word with him.

As she glided up the stairs so happy to be away from her cousins that breakfast was awful not the cooking, but the company.

She entered her room unbuttoning the pale blue day dress, she was reaching for her riding habit when Lilly breezed in "Sorry Miss I mean Amanda the massa kept me in the kitchens" "That's all right don't fret Lilly" Amanda said as she stepped out of the dress, Lilly unbuttoned the riding habit bodice as Amanda picked up the skirt stepping into it she buttoned the tiny pearl buttons on the side of the skirt then she slid her arms into the sleeves as Lilly held up the bodice then buttoned it.

She sat down at the dressing table to brush her hair as Lilly took the hat off of a shelf in the closet.

Lilly pulled her hair into a knot on top of her head then pinned the hat in place she spread the black ribbon that was tied around the hat out so that it hung down Amanda's back satisfied she stood thanking Lilly she left the room.

As she reached the base of the stairs she turned looking making sure her cousins were nowhere in sight she headed for the kitchens.

Della looked up surprised "Mornin' miss what can I do for you" "Um is um Cooper here" Amanda stammered "I'm afraid not Miss today is laundry day for us slaves so Cooper is gathering his clothes to wash" Della said conversationally as she bustled around the kitchen, "The house slave quarters are where exactly" Amanda asked nervously she felt like she was losing her nerve she wanted to run and hide somewhere, but she wanted to talk to Cooper that was the only thing holding her firmly in place, "Upstairs in the attic miss" Della said distractedly as she greased bread pans.

"Thank you Della" Amanda said cheerily as she turned and left the room, she took the stairs two at a time hoping that Cooper was still there.

As she reached the attic she saw Cooper coming down the ladder a basket in his hands, he cocked his head not really understanding what she was doing there "Miss Amanda" he said quietly his voice thick and deep it flowed over her like melted butter over bread.

"I wanted to talk to you Cooper, I wanted to see how you were feeling and to say I'm sorry for how you were treated I feel terrible, please say that you forgive me please" she said becoming more and more upset as she spoke, so upset that tears threatened to flow.

He smiled gently "Of course miss I'm fine why wouldn't I be please don't upset yourself" She stamped her foot "Stop it stop acting like a good slave Cooper tell me what you're thinking and feeling" she said her frustration growing Cooper frowned "Fine" he said his voice flat as he spoke "You want to know I'm angry I'm a slave I want out I want a life of my own that's how I am excuse me Miss I have work to do" he brushed passed her without another word.

The tears that threatened to fall now fell in earnest, she slid down the wall hugging her knees to her chest, she sat there for a long while, then she heard footsteps, but she just couldn't stop crying, Cooper stood watching her he blinked feeling bad "I made you cry miss didn't I" the shame evident in his voice, "I'm So sorry miss" "Cooper you have every right to be angry I would be too if I were kept in bondage, you seem like such a good person I only want to get to know you" she said gently the look on her face genuine as she spoke, he brushed a tear away holding it on his finger fascinated, it hit the floor with a silent splat, they looked at each other for a moment, blue eyes staring into green, then he moved it was sudden and graceful the way his body shifted he brushed his fingertips against her rounded chin tilting her face to meet his as his lips met hers, she slid her hand up into his hair feeling the stiff bristle of the short hairs against her palm she moaned against his mouth pulling him closer, he savaged her mouth pulling her close, then just as suddenly he broke the kiss saying quietly the shame and longing evident in his voice "I shouldn't have done that as much as I like you and want you you're to be the Big missy here the massa would kill me if they knew I touched you" She nodded then said "Cooper I don't want to be the Big missy if I had my choice I'd run away and not look back, I like you and want to be with you, I know I know this is crazy, but I want you to know that" she smiled kissing him quickly "By the way" she asked full of curiosity "What made you come back?" "I forgot something and I also felt bad about the way we left things, I was going to talk to you later if I got the chance" a bit of guilt in his voice.

He helped her up saying "I best go I have laundry to do" she nodded turning to go she smiled at him before heading down the stairs and out the door to the stables.

Cooper stood there a minute in bewildered silence she likes me he thought, she kissed me, she wants to be with me God if only I was free to do so, he grabbed the stock that he wore at the cotillion then he headed down the stairs to the slave quarters.

Amanda felt so free as she rode Arabella, pushing her into a run she flew through the high grass, her heart felt so light Cooper she thought what an amazing person he's steady as a rock, he's graceful and thoughtful, if only he were free she wondered if there was a way to free him, she'd have to think on it.

Lilly sat by the fire, she saw out of the corner of her eye Moe hobbling around she inwardly winced at the thought, she knew the sting of the lash she'd felt if herself on occasion "Moe" she said in what she hoped was a scolding tone "What are you doing you should be resting" Moe frowned "Since when do I have time to rest, the cotton gin needs fixing, Daddy's already over there so I need to go" she watched as Moe ambled out the door, she sighed standing up she walked to the door going outside into the yard she saw children at play and at work, then she saw Ol Jacob, he was sitting on the porch whittling, she knew he was leaving soon he'd been sold like his brother Ol Jeb she walked over to him sitting down beside him, she rubbed her damp palms on her skirt "I'm gonna miss you" she said her bottom lip quivering, he was like a grandfather to her he carved the most amazing things, "I know child" he said kindly patting her on the shoulder I'm gonna miss you too, alright give me a hug girl" he said trying to lighten the mood that had become so dark and somber.

She looked up as Cooper returned, she wondered what had gotten into him his smile was so bright and big surely something wonderful must've happened maybe the Massa's changed their minds and decided not to sell Ol Jacob.

"Boy what's gotten into you are you in love or something" Old Jacob asked with a wink in Lilly's direction, "She likes me too" he said so full of happiness he felt like bursting" "Amanda" Lilly breathed Cooper nodded and Old Jacob gave a low whistle "You going after the Massa's Big missy Cooper" he said as he shook his head "Your Mama would spin in her grave if she knew and not to mention your daddy what do you think he would say" Cooper looked at his shoes, he felt bad his father and brother were flogged just for talking to her he knew he should let her alone, let her go off and marry Massa Mervin even though she doesn't want to marry him, part of him felt like dying the thought of letting her go, but that was the best thing to do.

He nodded looking up "Your right ol' Jacob, it's for the best" Ol Jacob nodded as he handed them wooden spoons he'd finished carving, Lilly held hers to her chest knowing that she would never see Ol Jacob again and that she would miss him forever.

Cooper extended his hand for Ol Jacob to shake, he always liked and respected the older man as he put the spoon in his pocket, he'd use it later out of respect of the man.

Lilly went inside the cabin to check on the water, and then she came out nodding that it was ready.

A wagon suddenly pulled up a young slave a little more than a child was driving, an older portly gentleman in a moss green coat jump down from the passenger side, Hillcrest's foreman Michael Starr stepped forward hand extended "I'm pleased to meet you" he said trying to sound as professional as possible, Mr. Kent took his hand, but felt uncomfortable doing so Michael Starr had a reputation for cruelty as well as being known as white trash.

"Is this the slave Mr. Starr?" Mr. Kent asked "Yes, he is" Mr. Starr said proudly, he turned towards Old Jacob saying with definite superiority "Stand up boy your new owner is here" Ol Jacob stood slowly his head down in obedience, "Show me your teeth boy" Mr. Kent said seriously Ol Jacob ambled over opening his mouth wide, Mr. Kent slipped his gloves on grabbing Ol Jacob's chin he looked inside his mouth checking his teeth, "Show me your hands boy" Old Jacob showed him his hand palm side up and then turned them over, Mr. Kent nodded saying "Get in the wagon boy" "Yes Massa" Old Jacob said quietly as he walked over hopping up into the wagon, Mr. Kent said "Tell the McClure's I'll call on them soon, it's been a pleasure doing business with you Mr. Starr" he said with a smile then he jumped up into the passenger's seat, "Likewise Mr. Kent, and I'll tell the McClure's you stopped by" he said with a friendly smile, they both waved as the wagon started off.

The knot of slaves parted as Mr. Starr swaggered through, Cooper and Lilly looked at each other, Lilly's blue eyes blurred with tears and Cooper just felt sick knowing that they could be next.

Amanda continued her ride, she couldn't believe it Cooper really liked her there had to be a way, but was her excitement that made her so giddy, maybe they could run away together or she could buy him and then free him, hmmm she thought that was a possibility, but how to go about it. She rode until the horse was lathered and she was tired.

She headed back to the stables and then to the house for some lemonade and hopefully a sandwich.

As she left the stables she saw Cooper, he was walking up a well-worn path, and there were cabins back there she'd never noticed before, they were old, needed painting, and they were so small one room she thought, it would be very crowded for a family.

She lifted her skirts and ran to catch up with him; he stopped when he heard her approach, he turned his eyes brightened and his full mouth curved into a warm smile, he mentally kicked himself he was going to push her away and look he thought your welcoming her closer, this could be really bad for the both of them, he cleared his throat "Um hello" she smiled "Hello Cooper, I was riding and thinking and what if I bought you and then freed you is there a way I can do that?" He stood there dumbfounded was she serious, she seemed it, he felt like fainting, but maybe it was the heat. "I um yes there is a way you have to ask the Massa if you can buy me" she bit her lip "Mervin will ask why, he knows I like you" Cooper nodded disheartened she turned around feeling sick and scared. "Amanda" he asked uncertain "I'm alright" she said trying to sound brave "Mervin and Jonathan are powerful men, they scare me and their cruel" Cooper nodded "I know, you're just finding out how cruel and mean they are, I'm sorry you had to find that out" "Mother can be cruel in her own way" Amanda said quietly her thoughts in turmoil, so much to think about, poor Cooper she thought, she looked around at the rest of the slaves milling past and felt even worse, these are people and their being treated like animals, worse than animals.

"Well you best get to the Big House the Massas will wonder where you are?" Cooper said hoping that that little nudge would be enough to break the spell that was over them both.

She nodded looking around quickly, she turned and started to walk away, Cooper closed his eyes breathing deep, how he wanted to hold her, but he knew how impossible this all was, Amanda suddenly appeared back at his side saying" Don't worry I'll think of something" she smiled and walked away quickly, with her skirts lifted that way he could see a bit of her ankles, he grinned thinking about how extraordinary she is and how beautiful.

He made his way back to the Big House, in time to serve tea to Amanda and Sunshine Morre who had called on Amanda, they chatted amicably Cooper served the tea never meeting the women's eye, "Will that be all Miss?" Cooper said in a servants tone, Amanda flinched at his tone she frowned saying quietly "Yes, thank you Cooper" Sunshine eyed her suspiciously pursing her lips till Cooper left the room, "Alright Amanda talk to me, I'm your friend at least I hope you consider me to be a friend" Amanda bit her lip "I do consider you a friend, you can't tell a soul if I tell you, promise me Sunshine" Amanda said nervously Sunshine nodded saying excitedly "I promise" Sunshine moved to the settee where Amanda sat taking her cup with her, she sat demurely down balancing the cup in one hand.

Amanda took a breath letting it out slowly, where to begin she thought.

"I don't want to marry Mervin" she blurted Sunshine's eyes widened "I was sent here to marry him, but I don't want to" she ended on a teary note she pulled the handkerchief from her pocket, she dabbed at her eyes.

Sunshine patted her hand in genuine friendship and sisterhood, "It Cooper that you like isn't it" Sunshine said knowingly, Amanda nodded as her breath hitched in her throat making it impossible to talk.

"You do know the rumor don't you about their mother right" Sunshine said trying not to sound gossipy Amanda shook her head slowly, "Well rumor has it that their mother Betty was half white and that's why they appear to be white"

Amanda frowned "Lilly mentioned that, she also said that their mother was the master's favorite, you don't think that my cousin could be Cooper and Lilly's actual father, their father is Big Zeek" she said her hysteria rising.

Sunshine looked down at her hands as she said quietly "men do that with slave women, it's just the way it is, My Alan, you know I love him dearly, but he has fathered two children on two different slave women" Amanda was shocked, but then she saw that Sunshine understood and relaxed, "And you don't hate him for it?" Amanda asked curiously "I was upset when I found out, but then I got over it and realized that he loves me and wanted me to know, so I expect it" Amanda was impressed this is the friend she should have a strong confident woman, maybe together they could figure out a way for her to leave.

Amanda bit her lip as she said nervously" If I asked you to help me get away would you help me?" Sunshine looked surprised but nodded "Of of course" she stammered "But what can I do?" "I don't know yet, but I I mean we'll think of something" Amanda said as she felt more confident now that she had an ally.

They sipped their tea knowing that a true friendship had been born, and Amanda felt like she had to find out more about Jonathan and his possible relationship to Cooper.

The two women walked the grounds and gardens after tea, they talked about the goings on of the county.

All the while Amanda's mind ticked away, thinking that her own cousin could have fathered Cooper, they did look quite a bit alike, the same blue eyes, the same strong chin, and there was something else that she couldn't quite put her finger on, she'd figure it out eventually.

Amanda and Sunshine sat down to dinner, they were waiting on the McClure's, the two women had talked the day away, she hated the thought of Sunshine leaving later, but she knew she had to be strong.

Amanda looked up as the McClure's entered the room Mervin's eyes immediately sought Amanda's cleavage, he stared greedily at her Amanda tried her hardest to ignore Mervin and his greedy eyes. She wondered how she could find out if Cooper and Jonathan were related, maybe Della would know she's probably been here quite a while or maybe she could ask Big Zeeke, but how to go about it without insulting the man. She felt like this was important and the right thing to do, they deserved to know and she needed peace of mind.

She stood as if to stretch her legs and then she walked off towards the kitchens.

The air was warm in the kitchens, but smelled so good and was comforting, it reminded her of home and their cook Sherrilyn; the bright eyed red haired Irish cook her father had hired when he was still a bachelor she was sweet and always willing to try new recipes, her husband Michael and their son Rufus worked in the stables.

She paused in the doorway biting her lip and she fought to control her nervousness, how could she ask her about this kind of thing, Della looked up from her rolling pin "Miss Amanda" she asked questioningly "Um hello Della" she said nervously "Um I wanted to ask you something, its kind of personal, but I figured you would probably know about it "I'll do whatever I can to help you Miss Amanda" Della said kindly "Well you see I was talking with Sunshine, Miss Morre and she mentioned that sometimes slave owners take their slave women to their beds, has anything like that happened here" Amanda said.

Della scratched her head as she decided what to say Della knew all too well about the Massas and their appetites, there was a time when Massa Jonathan had sought her attentions. She was so glad those days were over, she had given birth to a stillborn girl child and Massa Jonathan was discussed that the child didn't live and never sought out Della again, she married of course and had healthy children that lived, but she never forgot that girl child, Abby she had called her.

Part of her wanted to tell the girl the very hard truth and part of her knew the penalties of that truth. "Sometimes men white men do seek out us slaves for their pleasures, but you needn't worry Massa Mervin loves you and wants to make you his wife and you will be his only love, so don't worry child."

Amanda smiled because she could sense that's what Della wanted her to do, she thanked her as Della poured her a glass of lemonade and set a dish of cookies in front of her.

Amanda sighed would she ever know the truth.

Maybe she should talk to Big Zeeke, but she hated the thought of hurting the man he'd been kind to her even though he'd been flogged on a count of her so maybe he wouldn't talk to her afterall.

She walked back into the dining room where Sunshine and the McClure's sat playing cards "You seem restless my dear are you alright?" Jonathan asked an eyebrow raised "Oh I'm fine Cousin Johnathan just fine, just thinking about something, I think I'll go to the library and find a good book to read" she said as she hoped her heart would stop racing she was so nervous, she needed to slow her heart rate, she walked from the room, she leaned against the wall letting out a deep breath she placed a trembling hand over her heart as she walked quickly to the library which Jonathan also used as his office.

She moved to the desk opening drawers.

She sorted through papers trying to find out anything about Cooper and Jonathan.

Her fingers hit the bottom of the drawer finding only wood, till the bottom of the drawer flipped up revealing a hidden drawer where several books lay.

She flipped through them recognizing Jonathan's handwriting, she realized that this could be what she was looking for, she left the room moving to the stairs where she made her way to her room to hide the books.

Amanda made her way back to the library where she grabbed a book off the shelf before heading back to the dining room, where she found that they had moved to the parlor where the card game was still in full swing and it looked like Sunshine was winning. Sunshine's wide grin caught Amanda's attention as she entered the room, Mervin laid a card down then picked one up off the pile he grimaced as he looked at the card before putting it in his hand.

Amanda sat down in the green and white overstuffed chair she spread the cinnamon colored gown around herself as she opened the book.

"What book did you get Amanda?" Sunshine asked as she laid a card down, Amanda blinked, she didn't know she'd just grabbed and left she looked at the book in her hands "Oh The Odyssey" she said trying not to sound guilty, "Oh that's a good book" Sunshine said cheerily as she laid her cards down in a fan on the table saying "Gin" both men frowned a little as Jonathan shuffled the deck for another game.

Amanda mind wandered as she read the books upstairs under her bed there's so much she wanted to know and she couldn't wait to find out.

The story of the Odyssey started to unfold before her eyes as she read she blocked out everything but the book.

She looked up an hour later as Sunshine touched her shoulder, she realized it was time for her to go home.

"Goodbye Amanda" sunshine said with a touch of sadness, Amanda stood and hugged her new friend saying "Goodbye I had so much fun today we need to do this again" "Of course" Sunshine said with a smile the two women embraced again laughing as they walked to the door arm in arm.

The men walked behind as they made their way to the door, where Cooper stood his back straight his hand on the doorknob.

Jonathan stepped behind Sunshine her shawl in hand, he slid it around her shoulders "Thank you Mr. McClure" she said genteelly, she then walked out the door and to the waiting carriage that will take her home to Maple field, her family's plantation.

Amanda turned towards her cousins' as she said "Well I'm going to head to bed I'm really tired, thank you for a lovely evening Cousin Jonathan, Cousin, Mervin" "Of course my dear you're welcome, sleep well my dear" Jonathan said as he patted her shoulder, she headed towards the stairs and her room.

Once inside the room Amanda raced to the bed where she dropped to her knees digging under the bed she located the journals she put them on the bed, then she walked to her the mirror where she sat and started taking the pins from her hair.

She had just started to brush her hair when Lilly breezed in "I'm so sorry" she breathed "Della needed help in the kitchens, I can help you get ready for bed" "Thank you Lilly" she said with a smile, she was so glad for Lilly's friendship and trust, should she tell her about the journals she didn't want to get Lilly in trouble, but she needed to tell someone she wet her lips that suddenly became dry "Lilly if I tell you something will you promise not to tell" Amanda said nervously Lilly blinked surprised "Of course Amanda, you can trust me" Amanda smiled relieved, she stood up walking to the bed she picked up the journal handing it to Lilly "It's my cousin's journal, it took them" Lilly's blue eyes widened she opened her mouth then closed it pursing her lips she said "What do you plan to do with them?" "Read them and find out a way to get out of this marriage, by black mailing them what do you think" Lilly's mouth dropped open in shock "Really" she said surprised Amanda nodded smiling wolfishly, it felt good to fight back.

"I'll tell you what I find out alright" Lilly nodded as she helped Amanda remove her dress and put on her nightgown and robe they sat down on the bed opening the first journal she started to read aloud.

9/10/1822

My name is Jonathan Simon Michael McClure, my mother Annabelle Keegan McClure suggested that I keep this journal

71

as my private thoughts and feeling are important and should be expressed and written down and preserved for all eternity.

An important thing happened today, I met the most beautiful woman ever her name is Betty and she's a slave, I will bed her she will be my bed warmer.

My father bought her from the Reverend Jackson's plantation in Mississippi my father told me that the Reverend is her father with a slave named Maddy, she has long curly dark brown hair and hazel eyes, she's perfect just perfect.

9/15/1822

Today was my first opportunity to be alone with Betty, I met up with her by the well she was so nervous that she dropped the bucket that she carried she apologized bowing her head dutifully, I told her to get more water and I would forget it, once she had the water she set the bucket down to wipe the hair from her eyes, I moved forward slowly so as not to frighten her grabbing her I kissed her she squirmed in my arms wrenching her mouth away she said "Oh Massa Massa Jackson said that my purity was a gift from GOD and it was her duty to protect it."

I blinked how could this girl still be a virgin when most slave women were known to be loose with their favors.

I kissed her again and she started to cry, she pushed passed me grabbing the bucket she headed for the house.

9/17/1822

The worst day of my life is here my father betrothed me to Angelica Thompson, she's pudgy round and plain, but her father has rich farmland and a lot of money, she is her parents only child so she's sure to inherit, but that's all she has going for her.

I prefer a tall slender woman like Betty.

I found out from her papers that she's 18 and in excellent health, father bought her to be the new kitchen girl as Della continually says she needs more help.

Why oh why couldn't father have betrothed me to one of the Stockdale girls Ginny was considered the Belle of the county and gentle and sweet to boot.

Maybe Angelica won't want me I can only hope.

Maybe she's heard about my wildness or that I like slender women, maybe I should try to be even more unpredictable, maybe she won't want me then.

My only saving grace for now is that she's too young to marry just yet.

My plan is to continue to try to get Betty in my bed, I'm getting tired of Della, not that she's not a good bed companion it's just that I want Betty.

Amanda looked up from the book she now understood her cousin Johnathan a little better he was in an unwanted marriage so why was he fighting so hard to stick her and Mervin together, maybe he didn't know that she didn't want to marry Mervin maybe if she told him he would call off the wedding and she could go home and forget about a of this, she just wanted to live her life and maybe find a fine gentleman that would marry her for her and not because of the fact that she was a Indigo heiress.

She looked over at Lilly who had a strange look on her face, "Lilly, are you alright?" Lilly blinked saying "I didn't know what she was like she died having me, she was a good person raised by a good Christian man even if he was her Massa he loved her and wanted her to be good" Amanda nodded "Of course" she held her friend close hoping that Lilly could find solace in the new information that she now had, she was sure that Lilly would tell Cooper she wished she could comfort him as well when he found out, she didn't know how much he remembered about his mother, he was probably young when she died.

"Lilly how old was Cooper when your mother died?"

"Don't know Amanda, I know that Cooper is in his 20's now and I'm in my late teens"

Amanda couldn't believe it they didn't know how old they are how odd she thought, "Oh" she said "maybe we'll find out maybe cousin Jonathan wrote it down somewhere" she turned to find the other journals Lilly put a hand over hers saying "We'll leave that for another time you best get some rest" Amanda nodded putting the journals back under the bed she smiled saying "Our secret" Lilly nodded as she turned down the covers so Amanda could crawl in bed, she snuggled down under the downy quilts as Lilly turned down the lamp then left the room.

Amanda stared at the dark ceiling her mind spinning with all she'd found out she knew it would be difficult to get any sleep so she let her mind wander till it exhausted itself and she fell into a deep sleep.

Lilly climbed the stepped to the servants quarters, she passed Coopers' bed and saw him sitting on the bed pulling off his shoes, "Cooper" she said quietly he looked up surprised to see her "I wanted to tell you before I return to Miss Amanda's room to sleep" "What what's going on is Miss Amanda alright?" he asked concerned "Oh she's fine Coop don't worry, she took her cousin's journals and she read them and found out about our mother, she was quiet and shy and a good christian woman, and Massa Jonathan wanted to bed her did you know that do you remember what she was like?" "That's good, she was quiet, how do you know she was a christian?" Cooper said interested "Her Massa was a reverend and he was also her father" Lilly said "Really what was his name?" Cooper asked "Massa Jackson, he was from Mississippi" "I remember her saying this is how we did this in Mississippi and she would do something and then smile in her quiet way, I remember she would always speak in a quiet way and she was gentle and loving, is that what you were wondering Lil" Cooper said with a smile and a teasing twinkle in his eyes.

She nodded feeling like she knew her mother a little better, smiling she stood kissing Cooper on the forehead she turned and left the room heading back to Amanda's room and to her own pallet on the floor.

As the sun rose Lilly woke sitting up she slid out of bed she stretched and yawned, she picked up her dress from where it was neatly folded on the chair, she crawled into it buttoning the buttons on the bodice of the navy blue dress, she walked to the window pulling up the shutters so the sun would shine in, she breathed as she knew that she would have battle

Amanda again, she shook her head as she thought about how tough it was to get Amanda out of bed.

Amanda stepped off the last step walking into the dinning room she noticed her cousin Johnathan sitting in the chair buttering a piece of toast, she smiled feeling a new sense of closeness to her cousin.

She sipped her tea as Cooper came around with a tray of biscuits, he kept his gaze off her only because he didn't want to upset the Massas as he left the room he stole glance at her, her long blond hair in a tight knot at the back of her head, the green dress with the white collar he smiled the green matched her eyes perfectly.

"What are your plans for today my dear" Jonathan said as he forked a piece egg stuffing it into his mouth, Amanda wiped her mouth on her napkin before she spoke "Well I've been enjoying the book the Odyssey so much I haven't read it in forever I thought I'd sit in the garden and read" Jonathan nodded "Well that would be fine for a while, but we really should discuss the wedding plans I think, don't you" Jonathon said an eyebrow raised Amanda lowered her eyes nodding "Your very right cousin, I do have a request though, it's always been my mother's dream that I wear her wedding dress and I neglected to bring it with me, might I go and get it" she asked sincerely.

Jonathan smiled it was all coming together as he planned all he had to do was get her money and he could stop selling slaves and live a good life with his grandchildren around his knees.

"Of course my dear I'll make arrangements, you'd best write to your mother and let her know"

Jonathan said a smug smile on his face.

Mervin looked at his father his grin broadened as he realized he'd have Amanda in his bed soon.

Amanda left the dinning room as soon as she could that was so uncomfortable she knew she'd have to escape and soon or she'd be married to Mervin.

She paced her room to knot in her stomach tightened even more, she wondered if she should ask Lilly and Cooper to come with her when she escaped, she knew they didn't like being slaves maybe she could get them to freedom in Canada, she'd ask Lilly to see what she thought.

She grabbed the journals heading down to the gardens maybe she could find something in the journals to hold over her cousins heads and maybe just maybe they would let her leave, but she realized that it would have to be when she went to get her mother's wedding dress that she could leave and not come back.

She reached the stone bench setting the journal's down she sat herself spreading her skirts around her she picked up a journal flipping through.

12/24/1822

I was forced by my father to dance with Angelica, she's a fair dancer, but she's not who I would pick I was forced to kiss her under the mistletoe when I stepped on her skirts. It was a pure accident on both accounts I swear it.

I put a mental image of Betty in my head before I kissed her.

After the dance I found Betty alone and kissed her proper, she was so distracted by my kiss that she didn't notice till it was too late that I'd got my hand under her skirt

She is a virgin or at least she was by the time I was through with her she was begging me to take her.

Amanda closed the book shaken as bile climbed up her throat poor Betty she thought.

Amanda opened the book still feeling ill, it opened to 1824.

5/24/1824

Betty gave birth today to her first child, she claimed the child was mine, but you know how slaves are, they have low morals everyone knows that.

Why not two days before she gave birth I saw her talking with a new slave named Big Zeeke, so he could be the father for all I know.

5/26/1824

I saw the child today his eyes are blue as blue as my own, I'm afraid he could be mine.

What will my parents say if they knew.

A twig snapped and Amanda looked up sharply to see Lilly standing there, Amanda smiled guiltily, "I was just reading more of the journals, I found out when Cooper was born" Amanda said with a smile, "Really, how old is he" Lilly asked excited "He's 26, he was born May 24ᵗʰ 1824" she said as she saw the look on Lilly's face it was childlike excitement, she felt bad this is something he should have known all along, it's sad that he didn't know.

She read aloud to Lilly what she had discovered, Lilly blinked shocked to her very core. No that can't be right she thought Big Zeke is my father, she knew that everyone did, she suddenly felt sick at the knowledge that her father might not be her father, "Cooper will want to know that too" Lilly said quietly Amanda frowned "I'm sorry Lilly, I was surprised too, my own cousin hurting your poor mother like that all I can say is I'm sorry" Lilly hugged her tightly as she said "I know Amanda, I know" and the women sat back wiping tears away.

"I wonder when I was born and how old I am?" Lilly asked as she pulled the hanky from her pocket" "Well we could find out" Amanda said trying to sound cheery, she flipped through the journal till she came across 1833.

2/23/1833

Betty gave birth to a baby girl today, she died bringing that girl child into the world, I can't believe she's gone, she bled to death, the child just wouldn't turn and she just bled and bled, the shock is more than I can bare, Angelica is angry with me she knows that I've bedded Betty and she's angry, but Mervin is my boy my heir so that's what matters I'll try to put Betty from my mind for the sake of my boy.

2/25/1833

Betty was buried today, Angelica knows that I was at the funeral and she's threatening to leave me, I won't let her take my boy, she can go if she wants too, but she can't have my boy.

3/1/1833

Angelica left me, she left her son as well, I came home from the fields with Mervin on my shoulders to find her gone Esther said that Angelica told her to pack and Aaron the stable boy packed her and her belongings into a carriage and they left.

I questioned Aaron when he arrived home and he said she boarded a ship for France, Aaron said she walked up the gangplank and didn't look back and the ship sailed away, Aaron said that she would write when she got settled, he said that's all he knows.

The nerve of that fat little thing, she can't do this to me I own her, well I won't let her get away with this.

3/51833

The girl child that took my Betty was named Lilly, Big Zeeke poor man is in shock,

I'll make sure he marries again quickly. Poor man three children to raise and no woman he'll marry again.

Amanda looked up as she heard a sniffled come from Lilly "I kilt her, my mama, she's dead cuz of me" Amanda grabbed her hand in true friendship and sisterhood "It wasn't your fault Lilly not really" Amanda said gently Lilly sniffled again a tear slid from her eye hitting her apron with a splash "Try not to think about it, wipe your face you'll feel better" Lilly pulled out her hanky wiping her face she took a deep cleansing breath feeling better somehow.

"I think I've bought myself a little more time, I told my cousins that I can't marry without my mother's wedding gown,

I told them that I'd have to go and get it, I won't be back, I wish I could take you with me you're my friend "Amanda said near tears she choked them back, but the lump was still there and she could barely swallow past it, "I wish I could take you with me, I hate the very thought of you being a slave" Lilly smiled nodding "I know Amanda believe me I know" "Did your father ever remarry?" she asked curiously "Oh yes her name is Cora, she's a good person" "Amanda blinked "Cora oh yes the downstairs maid with the green cloth tied in her hair". Lilly nodded "She lives in the second to the last hut" Amanda blinked in surprise "They don't live together?" "No Daddy says Mama was his one true love and he can't betray her, she shacked up with Peter one of the field hands they seem very happy together" Amanda was so surprised by what Lilly had told her.

"Cooper will be sad to see you go, he cares for you" Amanda nodded she'd been thinking about that.

"I'll miss him too, you both are very special to me" she choked back another sob, Cooper was very special to her too, his image floated before her eyes and she couldn't block him out she sighed her stomach churning, she wanted to be with him what am I going to do she thought.

Cooper sat at the table polishing the silver, occasionally he would look out the window towards the gardens.

Della raised an eyebrow as she passed the table, Cooper lowered his eyes blushing, Della chuckled as she came up behind him, "God love you Cooper, what a good man you are if only you could have her" "I know she belongs to the Massa, I do, but I can't help it, I can't help what I feel" Della nodded kissing the top of his head with motherly affection as she waddled passed the butter crock held tightly in her chubby fingers.

As noon neared Cooper came out to the gardens to announce luncheon, the two women looked up in surprise.

"Oh" Lilly said "Tell Della I'm sorry, I'll come in and help her" Cooper nodded then turned away, walking in that slow steady gait, his back ever straight.

Lilly raced into the kitchens, washing her hands in the bucket, she dried them quickly on her apron before opening the soup tureen and ladle in the beef soup that Della had prepared.

Amanda sat gracefully in the chair as Cooper served the soup, she smiled quietly at him as he came around with the soup.

"Thank you Cooper" she said sweetly, he nodded saying "My pleasure miss" after he had ladled out the soup he left the room as quietly as he came in.

Jonathan eyed her saying "Have you written to your mother yet?" she knew he was trying to be conversational but, she knew he was pushing her.

"I was going to write after luncheon" she said with a sweet as sugar tone that she didn't feel, she hated being pushed she wished Da was alive, he would never put her through this.

"Very good dear" Jonathan said as he spooned the soup into his mouth, he was trying very hard to keep his temper in check he knew she was stalling, but why, he need that money didn't she get it that she was a pawn and means to an end all women were, did she think he wanted to marry Angelica, she had money she made him richer.

He wondered what game she was playing, but he knew she wouldn't win.

Amanda sat at the writing desk, she tapped the pen against her teeth, paper littered the floor, she'd started and threw away so many letters, she hoped she'd get it right.

She bent her head and started to write.

7/18/1850

Dearest mother,

I am writing to let you know that I'm coming home to get your wedding dress, I know that you've always dreamt of me wearing it for my own wedding.

All my love,
Amanda

She carefully folded the letter and sealing it in an envelope, she stood walking towards the door when she heard the most horrific scream rent the air she ran cautiously looking out, Lilly ran from her cousin Johnathan office and up the stairs her dress was ripped in several places and her nose was bleeding, Jonathan moved like a tiger taking the stairs two at a time "Get back here girl" he said in a deadly whisper "I'm not through with you yet" Lilly cowered in the corner "Cousin Jonathan?" Amanda said confused he blinked in surprise at seeing her then frowned "This is none of your affair Amanda go back to your room" he said sternly.

Amanda ran down the stairs shouting Cooper's name as she went, as she entered the kitchens she met Rhea "Where's Cooper?" she said her voice shaking "He's out back by the well" she said "Hurry run and get him" Amanda said in a panicky voice Rhea ran out the door.

Amanda lifted her skirts running back to see what she could do for Lilly, as she reached the top of the stairs she saw her cousin with a riding crop beating Lilly across the back.

Lilly lay curled in a fetal position, her sobs could be heard over the whistling of the riding crop.

Cooper came up behind her shouting "No, Massa don't!" he moved passed trying to shield his sister from the blows.

He suddenly reached up grabbing the riding crop from Jonathan's hand, he stood slowly purposefully his graceful stance now hard and unbending as he swung the riding crop hitting Johnathan across the face bleeding it, Cooper's eyes blue ice as he moved the riding crop whistling through the air Johnathan crumpled under the assault.

Amanda moved to Lilly's side taking the handkerchief from her pocket she wiped the blood from her face.

Amanda looked over at Cooper saying "Cooper that's enough" she stood grabbing his arm, he turned blinking at her the rage suddenly melting from his eyes, "I couldn't let him do it no more" he said his face crumpling his breath hitched in his throat as he turned toward Lilly who now stood on shaky legs, she leaned against the wall her arms out stretched, Cooper moved towards her "No Cooper you have to run now you beat the Massa you're a dead man, go run, live for both of us" she said as tears burned her eyes.

Cooper pulled Amanda to him kissing her hard and quick leaving her breathless, "I'm sorry Amanda for all of this" he said with regret she put her fingers to his lips saying "Never regret our love" she smiled sadly he kissed her fingers "Never" he said with a smile kissing her again he ran for the servants stairs.

He grabbed his clothes putting them in his pillow case he ran down the stairs meeting Zeeke on the stairs "The word is out you need our protection" Zeeke said matter of factly he ussered Cooper down the stairs and out the back door to the cotton shed "Daddy I don't have time for this I have to run" he said urgently Zeeke held up a hand saying "You will when it's safe to do so, but for now let us protect you" Cooper nodded as they entered the shed.

"Remember when we built the new cotton shed?" Zeeke asked Cooper nodded confused "Well a group of us came back and built a secret room for runaway slaves" Moe said as he slid the wall out revealing the hidden room, Cooper blinked in surprise as he stepped into the room "We'll be back later with food and water take care my brother" Moe said with pride, he slid the wall back in place.

The two men continued their work on the cotton gin as Mervin burst in, "Where is he?" he shouted the two men looked up in surprise "Where is who massa?" Zeeke asked in innocence Mervin slammed Zeeke against the wall making it rattle he grabbed the older man around the throat shouting "Cooper where is he?" "I don't know massa" Zeeke said in wide eyed innocence.

Mervin growled stalking away Michael Starr moved out the door behind him, Moe stuck his head out glancing first to the left and then to the right then he pulled his head back in and nodded.

Zeeke open the door, Cooper ran out his mouth open Zeeke put a hand over his mouth whispering "Sh, don't speak, We'll tell you when it's safe for you to leave you have to trust us now" Cooper nodded walking back inside and the door was slid in place.

Amanda went Zeeke the next day.

"Zeeke, is he safe, is he alright?" She cried

Zeeke nodded, "He's fine, come later tonight and I will show you.

She nodded hurrying away.

She entered the Big house, she started up the stairs, she would've gone to her room if she hadn't heard her cousin scream.

Amanda ran to his room knocking on the door "Cousin Johnathan are you alright?"

"Go away" came a shouted reply, Amanda sighed as she opened the door.

It was dark and smelled of blood, "Cousin Johnathan?"

"Why are you here?" Jonathan growled, "I- I - I wanted to help you if I could" "That was just terrible what happened, I would never want that to happen you must believe me."

Jonathan shifted restlessly in the bed, there was a bandage covering most of his face, his blue eyes glared out at her from the bandage.

Amanda stared out the window, it was just getting dark.

Zeeke should be coming soon.

Amanda paced the room.

A sounded on the door to Amanda's room.

She answered it, it was Cora.

"Zeeke's waitin' down stairs Miss" Amanda nodded "Thank you Cora"

The two women left the room.

Amanda walked out onto the porch, Zeeke waited in the shadows "Miss Amanda. Come with me. Promise me you won't repeat anything about what you see here."

"Promise. Is Cooper alright"

"He's fine, thank you for asking Miss Amanda"

They walked across the yard to the cotton shed.

Zeeke opened the cotton shed door walking towards the back.

He opened a false wall.

Cooper stood up when the wall opened.

"Cooper, you're alright" Amanda squealed as she ran to hug Cooper.

"Amanda" Cooper held her close kissing her soundly.

"Can we have some time alone?"

Zeeke nodded closing the door.

They kissed again passionately as they moved to the cot.

"I think I've found a way to get you to safety"

"How?"

"I've written to my mother, I told her that I want to wear her wedding dress, I've had a chest made with sliding panels, you and Lilly can hide in there."

"Really, you want to help us"

"Yes, I do, I care about you and Lilly"

"I know, I just wanted to hear you say it" Cooper laughed.

Amanda laughed, Cooper swung her around, they landed on the cot in a puff of skirts.

"I want you for my own Amanda" Cooper said seriously Amanda kissed him.

He slid his hands along side her breasts and down her ribcage his thumbs coming to rest under her breasts, his thumbs massaging her nipples, her head fell back under all the sensation, her mouth opened as she panted slightly.

Cooper moved his hands to the back of her dress he unbuttoned it sliding it from her slight shoulders, her flesh was a rosy cream he could see a slight bluish tint of the veins beneath the surface.

Her breasts were large and perfectly tipped if what he saw through the material of her camisole was any indication, his mouth watered for a taste.

He leaned in for a taste, licking his way around the creamy globes, she panted tossing her head wildly "More more" she panted, he removed her dress tossing it to the floor.

He moved her closer on his lap then he layed her down gently moving over her, he slid her underskirts up as moved.

There it was right in front of him her downy blond womanhood.

He wanted her, but she was a virgin and that he would hurt her and he didn't want to hurt her, she was gentle, sweet and innocent, he knew that Massa Mervin wouldn't be gentle he would hurt her and bad.

He wanted to take her away, but there was no where he could go.

He kissed her gently, he cupped her head as he kissed her more passionately, she wrapped her arms around his neck pulling him close.

He suddenly sat up trying to think before he got himself in too deep, "Cooper?" she asked uncertain he ran a hand through his short dark hair, he swallowed hard "I want you, but to do so will hurt you and I feel bad about hurting you" he said with remorse, Amanda smiled "That makes me love you all the more, I want to be yours Cooper make me yours" she said her eyes bright with love.

He laid her down kissing her hard, he bunched her dress in his fist pulling it up baring her lower half, he slid his hand across her stomach moving it lower his fingers brushed her golden mound, she arched unconsciously as he skimmed her slick folds she moaned low in her throat as he rubbed her nub, he parted his lips breathing raggedly as he got harder.

She parted her legs wider seeking more of the stimulation he provide, she writhed in pleasure, he lowered his pants his manhood swung free, Amanda's eyes widened as she saw him he was huge she didn't know how it would fit inside her, she bit her lip in worry Cooper stopped suddenly looking at her confused she smiled embarrassed she shook her head and kissed him back.

He laid her down into the scratchy wool blanket, he moved over her spread her legs wide he positioned himself at her entrance knowing that he would hurt her and it bothered him, but he wanted her as much as she wanted him.

He pushed himself inside her, she whimpered jerking, then she relaxed and arched her hips upward as she moved against him.

The passion returned and they moved together straining to reach fulfilment.

Amanda suddenly felt like a bubble was forming inside her and it kept expanding till it burst in white hot pleasure, she arched into him crying out, he nuzzled his face into her neck as he continued to moved against her he breathed in her floral scent he sighed then followed her over the edge into bliss.

He fell heavily on top of her both of them breathing hard "I'm yours now" she said happily, her eyes bright, Cooper smiled pulling her close saying seriously "Yes, yes you are mine" she kissed him touching his face.

"You best get back to the Big House", Amanda frowned knowing that he was right, but not wanting to leave yet.

He hated sending her away, but he knew he had to, keep her and Lilly safe, he hoped that when she married that she would believe that he loved her and that he always would.

He wanted to scream in rage at how unfair it was that he couldn't have her with him, that he would have to run soon and he hoped that he wouldn't be caught, but just in case he was he knew that Amanda would care for Lilly and his father and brother.

Cooper stood going over to the pitcher grabbing a cloth he poured water in the bowl dunking the cloth he cleaned himself then he rinsed the cloth and handed it to Amanda, she smiled accepting the cloth and cleaned herself.

They both dressed slowly not wanting this to end.

As she walked passed him she stood on her tip toes kissing him, he pulled her into his embrace kissing her back.

He broked the kiss nuzzling her neck breathing in her floral scent, Amanda put a hand in his hair sliding her fingers through the short crisp hairs, she laid her head against his, she wanted to stay with him here and now, but she knew she couldn't she would have to go back and sit, talk, eat, and be with Mervin, maybe she could say she wasn't feeling well and get out of it, she would cross her fingers.

She opened the door turning around she slid her fingers in his hair she kissed him quickly then she left.

She made her way up the path to the house.

She lifted her skirts running up the steps to her room, where she asked Cora to draw her a bath.

She slipped into the steaming water, she breathed deep of the steam and the rose oil that perfumed the water.

Lilly bustled in smiling "Cooper" she asked concerned Amanda smiled back "He's fine" "Lilly if I tell you something promise me you won't say anything?" she asked biting her lip, Lilly crossed the room kneeling in front of the tub "Amanda you know you can trust me, I'm trusting you with Cooper's whereabouts" Amanda nodded knowing that she was right.

"Cooper made me his" she blurted Lilly's eyes widened, she moved closer hugging Amanda, who layed her head on Lilly's shoulder "He loves you, you know that" Lilly said with a smile, Amanda straightened smiling "I love him too" she said her voice full of emotion.

"So how do you feel, do you feel different?" Lilly asked worried "I'm a little sore down there, but I'm so happy I can't even tell you."

Amanda said brightly.

As the afternoon wore on Sunshine flounce in when the door open, she wore a light blue dress.

Amanda ran down the steps and they hopped into a carriage and headed into town.

"I came to tell you that Massa Mervin is still out looking for Cooper" Lilly said Amanda smiled brightly feeling safe for awhile at least.

Mervin's anger grew as he headed farther into the woods.

He could hear the men of the posse behind him some them talked about what they'd like to do to Cooper when they found him, but most talked about going home to get their suppers'.

If they didn't want to help him they should just go home he thought, I can do this myself.

Mervin stood on the hillside in the growing dark.

The men behind him lighting lanterns.

The complaints were growing louder and Mervin's nerves were chafing, he clenched his fists to keep from striking the men he'd always called friends.

Amanda made her way down the hall to her cousin Jonathan's room.

She took a deep breath before she entered.

Jonathan lay in the bed bandages covered his arms and back, he slowly turned his head as she entered she tried to hide the grimace and the fear and the sickness that washed over her when she saw the bandage covering his one eye.

She gracefully sat in the chair by the bed, she arranged her skirts then clearing her throat said "How are you feeling Cousin Johnathan?" He sighed turning his head away, then he said with such contempt it made her shiver "Has Mervin caught the slave yet?" "I don't know he's not not back yet" she said quietly.

"When he does I want him hanged" Jonathan said vehemently.

Amanda gasped "Cousin Jonathan you can't what about taking him to court?" she cried Jonathan eyed her his gaze narrowing "He's a slave, he has no rights we hang em' when they misbehave, your lucky I'm letting you keep Lilly." Amanda felt sick, how was she going to get Cooper and Lilly out of this mess.

"Is there anything I can get for you Cousin Jonathan?" Amanda asked "Yes, you can ask Lilly where Cooper ran too, so I can kill him" Jonathan said angrily Amanda frowned "Cousin Johnathan, she doesn't know I think you've done enough to her Jonathan gave an evil laugh saying "Not nearly enough" Amanda let out her breath in a huff standing suddenly she left the room.

She couldn't believe she was related to people like that.

The very notion was repulsive to her, she had to get Cooper and Lilly away from here.

She'd talk to Sunshine and see what they could come up with.

Amanda walked down the hall to her own room.

Her stomach churning with all that she knew running around her head, it was so much.

She didn't feel ready for this jump into a larger world, part of her wanted to run and hide in her father's arm and ask him to make it all go away, but her Irish stubbornness just wouldn't let her.

Amanda reached her room, she entered turning up the lamp.

Sitting down at the vanity she removed the pins from her hair, then she stood to remove her dress and undergarment.

She wiggled into her nightgown then she crawled into bed to read more of her cousins' journals.

She hoped she could find away to help Cooper and Lilly.

Amanda woke the next morning with Lilly shaking her awake.

"Morning Amanda, sorry I didn't mean to wake you.

"No it's alright Lilly, I should be getting up anyway."

Sunshine flounced into the garden as Amanda read her cousin's journals.

Zeeke carried the chest in setting it against the wall, He then brought in a plate of food.

"What is that chest doing in here Daddy?" "Your Miss Amanda has a plan to help you and Lilly and that's part of it"

"Really, a chance at freedom and Amanda" Cooper said with a dreamy happy smile.

"I'll miss you son, my boy" sorrow hitting him hard.

"Come on we're going shopping" Amanda smiled jumping up. "Let me grab my bag."

She ran to her room setting the book on her bed, she grabbed her bag and left the room. The carriage pulled out of the driveway of Hillcrest. The two women walked down the street, people ran passed them towards the town square. The two women looked at each other and hurried towards the town square, where a slave auction was being held.

"You don't want to see this Amanda, trust me" Sunshine said seriously Amanda bit her lip as she saw the people on the auction block that awaited their fate.

A man walked up to the women, "I was hoping to stop that" he said the horror eveadent on his face.

"My name is Fredrick Douglas, I'm pleased to meet you ladies" he said kindly Amanda Green and I'd like you to meet Sunshine Morre"

"Come along ladies, you don't need to see to see this" The three people walked away "Mr. Douglas I wanted to ask you a question?" "Someone I care about is a slave, is there a way I can help them?" "Yes, get the person away from slavery as soon as possible"

As they walked Amanda saw the shop, and an idea started to form, she could smuggled them out in one of her trunks, all she would have to is find a way to make sure they could breathe.

What about sliding panels in the sides.

Perfect, she thought.

She would ask Big Moe and Big Zeke. When they arrived back at Hillcrest Amanda went back to the garden to read, till Lilly arrived.

Amanda sent a message to Sunshine about the chest that she had made.

SAVING COOPER

Zeeke hoisted the trunk on to the top of the carriage, Moe tossed the rope over the top of the carriage, they tied the trunk down securely, Zeeke laid a large dark scarred hand on the top of the trunk whispering "May God be with you" then he hopped lightly down, which was strange for a man of his size to be so light on his feet.

Cooper slid the small panel open letting the cool air rush in, Lilly bit her lip in fear as she slid the other panel open, she looked through trying to see Amanda, "I see her Lilly, Mandy wouldn't abandon us" Cooper said trying to reassure his sister, "I'm sho scared Cooper, what if the Massa won't let her leave" Lilly said as she fidgeted with her apron twisting it around her finger, Cooper laid a hand over hers stilling her hands.

Amanda stood on the steps her cousins stood behind her, Mervin stepped forward taking her hand, he kissed it, Amanda smiled tightly "I can't wait for us to be together my sweet, do you really have to wear your mother's wedding gown" Mervin said trying to sound sincere, Amanda nodded "It's tradition, I can't go against tradition, I will be back soon" she couldn't wait to be away from them and be with Cooper, oh Cooper oh to kiss him and make love to him, she hoped to marry him she thought as she walked with Mervin to the carriage, she stepped in closing the door, the driver flicked the reins and the carriage started off, it climbed the hilly swervy road, she had the carriage stopped near the bottom of the hill asking the driver to take the trunk down, the driver Rufus looked thoroughly confused, but took the trunk down anyway.

Amanda got out of the carriage walking over to Rufus she said "What I'm about to reveal to you, you have to swear that you'll never tell another soul as long as you live please Rufus this is important" Rufus nodded "Yes Maam" "Good" Amanda said with a smile.

Amanda opened the trunk and Cooper and Lilly stuck their heads out, Rufus looked totally thunderstruck "You took your cousins' slaves" Rufus said shocked "Yes, I did, I did it to save their lives, they'll have a better life and a fresh start in Pittsburgh, no one will ever hurt them again" Amanda said as she affectionately touched Cooper cheek he smiled stepping out of the trunk, they got into the carriage, Amanda had fine clothes waiting for them to wear, "I don't think we'll fool anyone, people will know" Cooper said as he straightened his tie looking nervous "No Cooper you're wrong you, the two you could pass for white, trust me" she said as she clasped their hands tightly, "I do trust you, we both do or else we'd still be slaves, you've given me so much Mandy you don't even know" Cooper said as he tried to blink back tears, he reached out pulling her close crushing her to his chest he kissed her soundly, she touched his face her fingers slid through the stubble on his face, "Don't bow or act like you're less than human look other people in the eye, you're free to do as you please act like it" Amanda said enthusiastically "To get married if I like" Cooper said with a smile as he brushed a strand of blond hair behind her shell like ear, "We should shouldn't we ....er I mean get married," Amanda gave him a covetous look "Are you asking Cooper?" Amanda inquired the blush crept up his neck suffusing his face, she kissed him "Yes, let's get married Mandy" she hugged him kissing him soundly "Yes, let's get married Cooper my love" he pulled her close, "Finally you two" Lilly teased.

Amanda nodded approvingly as Cooper stared at himself in the mirror, he looked good he thought dressed up as a fine wealthy gentleman.

Amanda payed the salesman as Cooper laid the clothes he was wearing on the counter "I'll wear these out my good man" he said smoothly, Amanda was proud of him his voice never wavered, he was getting used to being free she thought.

They walked out of the haberdashers Amanda's hand through Cooper's arm.

They strolled down the street to the carriage.

Lilly stood in front of a fountain, she stood in awe of the water bubbling up and cascading down, Cooper and Amanda strode up alongside her "Penny for your thoughts" Amanda said cheerily Lilly glanced over to her new sister in law with a smile "I was just thinking about all that has happened and that I'm so glad to be free" Amanda hugged her whispering "Me too dear sweet sister."

Cooper and Lilly stared out the window of the carriage in awe of the city of Pittsburgh, Pennsylvania.

As the carriage rolled up the curved driveway of the house that Amanda had grown up in.

Honey was surprised when Amanda, Cooper, and Lilly appeared in the doorway of her mother's study.

"Amanda, you've taken your cousins' slaves, Jonathan wrote to me he's sent men to bring them back, I shall write to him and tell him, he quite angry you know" She said disapprovingly "Mother please don't, they'll kill Cooper and do God knows what to Lilly, I have to protect them "she said stubbornly "Amanda" Honey exclaimed "There are laws, you know that they have to got back" "Oh stop it mother you'll give yourself a nosebleed" Amanda said tiredly.

May peeked around the doorway nervously she said "It's good to see you Miss Amanda" Amanda smiled "May it's good to see you as well, can you help me pack please" May nodded heading up the steps.

Honey stood in the doorway as they started down the stairs "Amanda I forbid you to go" she said sternly "Goodbye mother" she said calmly "Amanda" Honey shouted parentally as they headed back to the carriage and set out for a hotel.

Amanda sat at the writing desk at the hotel, she wrote to Mr. Douglas hoping he could help.

Several days later letter in hand Amanda read the letter that Mr. Douglas had written.

Amanda, Cooper, and Lilly walked slowly up the gangplank on the ship The Greenwood which was headed for Buffalo, Ny, from there they would head for Canada and freedom for the two former slaves.

The ship docked in Buffalo, Ny and Amanda hired a carriage to take them into Ontario, Canada and into the Village of Little Africa.

PROLOGUE

WINTER 1851

The cabin was warm and dry which was a contrast to the cold winter outside.

Amanda sat by the fire rocking the baby boy in the cradle, she looked down lovingly on her young son, he looked so much like Cooper, they named the baby Shamus after her father.

Amanda stood stepping around the knitting basket on the floor as she made her way to the door to greet her frozen husband.

He hung up his coat bending down to kiss Amanda soundly they walked to the cradle peering down affectionately on the sleeping baby.

Amanda made tea and ladled soup for their dinner.

As they ate they spoke of Lily's up coming wedding to Kenneth Willows and all the preparations that went along with a wedding.

Everyone was just exhausted.

Cooper withdrew a letter waving it merrily Amanda looked at it questioningly "It's from Mr. Douglas" Cooper explained "He's bringing Zeeke and Moe, he's gotten them to freedom" Amanda closed her eyes smiling when she opened them they were wet with tears "Oh Cooper that's wonderful I can't wait to see them."

Moe pushed his cap back as he scratched his bald head "So this is Dawn, the end of the journey" he asked questioningly as he stared at the muddy dirt and snow covered streets and small log cabins nestled among the tall pines, Zeeke didn't have time to reply as Cooper ran up hugging them both "Welcome home, come to the house and rest and eat Amanda can't wait to see you" the three men walked down the street to the cabin.

Amanda looked up from the table she was setting as the men came in, Lilly ran out of the kitchen letting out a happy squeal as she embraced both her father and brother.

"How did you like your conductor, Mr. Douglas he was so nice to us" Amanda said sweetly "He was very nice to us and our stations were very nice" Zeeke said "We passengers couldn't have asked for better" Zeeke smiled.

They sat down to eat Zeeke and Moe dreaming of the life of freedom that they now have thanks to the bravery of one woman.

The End

GLOSSARY OF TERMS

Massa- Master
Conductor- People who help slaves escape
Passengers- Slaves that escape
The underground railroad- A way to get slaves to freedom by
hiding them as they ran to freedom
Stations- rest stops
Dawn- the end of the journey

Printed in the United States
By Bookmasters